The Listener

By George Clement

Dedication

I dedicate this book to the Samaritans, who are there for us. Every minute, every hour, every day.

About the author

When my grandson committed suicide at the age of eighteen it understandably devastated my family. I made a pledge to try to stop this happening to other families, so I decided to join the Samaritans as a Listening Volunteer.

I managed to pass selection, which in itself was a great achievement, and completed the most thorough and comprehensive training programme I had ever experienced.

I have spent the last two-and-a-half years listening to not only suicidal people but all types of people, with all types of problems, who are desperate to talk to someone. It has been a wonderfully rewarding experience, full of emotion and sometimes tragedy. But I am glad I have been able to help.

I wanted to write an account of the types of calls I had received, whilst protecting the confidentiality of the callers. So my work of fiction, telling the story of Robert the Listener, was born. I am sure readers will find this book interesting.

Author's note

Mental health issues are being widely discussed in this modern age with people becoming more aware of this invisible illness; it has always existed but, in the not so recent past, was usually hushed up. Sufferers of this illness were sometimes referred to as 'nutters' or were cruelly described as being 'not quite the full shilling'. These days a certain amount of respect is shown to the victims of this affliction and we tend to display empathy rather than ridicule to those struggling with its devastating effects.

It is a fact that since the mid-1950s organisations have existed to offer support, not only to those of us who are mentally unwell but to all types of troubled people with a wide range of problems. To name just a few would include *Alcoholics Anonymous* and *Drink Line*, whose purposes are obvious, *Cruse* for the bereaved, *Shelter* for the homeless and, of course, the Samaritans, who were originally founded to offer support to suicidal people but are now there for anyone with a problem which they would like to discuss in private. There are probably more than one hundred other organisations who offer help to people with mental health or welfare issues. Most of these organisations have one thing in common: the personnel who work within them are all volunteers who give their time, day and night, to help others.

This novel is a work of fiction and tells a story of a few of the volunteers who man the phones in a charity that helps others. Anyone reading this book may ask what do I, the writer, know of such things and the answer is that I have had the honour of working with the Samaritans for almost three years as a Listening Volunteer and this is where I experienced the types of calls made by people with similar issues to the troubled characters who are portrayed in this book.

As stated, the novel, the Listening Organisation, the volunteers, the calls and the callers are all fictitious. However, the type and nature of the calls which are contained in this narrative are all too real in today's society.

Any serving or past Listening Volunteer with the Samaritans, or similar organisation, reading this book will be able to recognise these types of calls and admit that they are received all too frequently.

As such, the pervert, the lady who did not want to die alone, the jilted girlfriend, the Falkland Islands war veteran, the young mother driven to prostitution, the girl being controlled by her partner, the young mum next to the railway line, the grieving widower and all the rest of the calls outlined in this book are, and have been, reality issues for real-life Listening Volunteers.

All of the listening charities that exist today are a totally confidential and safe place for people to call who are feeling troubled and the volunteers, such as the Samaritan volunteers, are the unsung heroes of today's society. They are always there for the callers, every minute, every hour, every day.

I dedicate this book to all Listening Volunteers and I pledge to donate a part of any profits made through the sale of this book to the Samaritans.

George Clement, July 2019

Part One

'It's What We Do'

Prologue

September 2017

I had never known despair before. I had always been the eternal optimist, always looking at the future through rose-coloured spectacles. I had never lived a lifestyle that resembled some sort of latter-day James Bond. I lived my life more like the Dickensian character, Wilkins Micawber: "Something will turn up". Life had been good to me; it had been interesting and full of incident. All of these things were brought about and made to happen by my own unflinching selfishness.

I have always been in control of myself, my body and my mind. But that day, in 2017, my body was here under the tree where I sat but my mind was over there, under that next tree. I could feel my mind, but I was not in control. The voices were echoing in my ears telling me … telling me to end it all. They were in control of me; the voices.

My mind had left my body and I was in despair. I desperately wanted to regain possession of my mind; I was reaching out for it, grasping at it, but I was not in control and my mind was not with me. I could never fight the voices or anything else without ownership of my mind. It was hopeless.

This is the world of mental illness in which I suffered almost two years ago, in 2017. No one intends to become mentally ill, but millions of us do. There are no visible scars; people do not break out in a rash or walk with a limp when they experience mental health issues. It is an invisible illness, an illness that is more readily recognised now than it was then, even two years ago.

I had spent the previous two-and-a-half years helping people cope with their illnesses, pulling them back from despair, from the brink of disaster. Then, all of a sudden, out of the blue, I became a victim.

Many people who are suffering from mental health issues contact a helpline, particularly the Samaritans, in their desperation.

This is what happened to me.

Chapter One

London, June 2017

My telephone was ringing, but the sound was muted, as though someone had smothered the device with a blanket. A muffled electronic warbling was alerting me to the fact that yet another member of the public needed to share a problem with me. Loud noises were not required here in this small and intimately quiet call centre, where I was sat waiting for my callers. The red indicator light was flashing on my console, a beacon glowing brightly with each ring, beckoning me to answer. I looked out of the window and down at the empty High Street of the London Borough of Welford. At four in the morning the street was totally deserted but, over the roof tops, signs of the impending dawn were visible. Daylight arrived early in beautiful British summertime, during the golden month of June.

I was supposed to answer the telephone on the third ring but I allowed it to continue; I was weary, I had been on duty since 2am and I was yet to receive a really meaningful call. A drunken Glaswegian whose strong accent mixed with the drink was impossible to understand, a sex caller looking for a female listener, a lady whose cat was missing and an inmate at one of Her Majesty's prisons, wanting a chat to alleviate himself of the soul-destroying boredom that he was suffering whilst incarcerated, were the calls I had received so far. I looked around the small room. My shift buddy was bent over her desk with the phone receiver pressed to her ear and her long brown hair seemed to glisten under the desk lighting. Nicola was totally absorbed in her caller, impervious to my stare. I dragged my mouse to the 'Take Call' box on my computer screen and clicked on it. My headset crackled once as the ringing tone stopped and I adjusted the integral microphone, moving it closer to my mouth, as I said, "Can I help?"

It was the same greeting every time. All of my fellow Listeners said the same thing. We never answered the telephone by announcing our organisation's name. If a person had taken the trouble to dial our freephone number, 333444, they would know who they were phoning? Wouldn't they?

"Hello," the caller said. It was a male voice.

"Can I help?" I repeated quietly.

"Hello, are you one of those Listeners?" It was a male voice with a north-eastern accent.

"Yes, that's right," I replied, in a fairly cheerful tone; we were trained to make the callers relax.

"How can I help?"

"I canna sleep," stated the caller.

"Oh, really. I'm sorry to hear that." I really hoped that this was a genuine caller.

"Is there anything in particular that's causing your sleeplessness? Anything you would like to talk about?"

"Well it's embarrassing like." He was mumbling and breathing heavily. I sighed an inner sigh and thought, *Oh dear, here we go*. I was thinking that this may not be a genuine call after all. Gut instinct and experience told me that. My training, however, has taught me never to prejudge, so I continued our dialogue.

"Okay. Is it possible for you to tell me what it is that you are you finding embarrassing? You don't have to, but maybe you will find it helpful to talk about it."

"Well I could, but it's embarrassing."

Bloody hell, I thought to myself, *we're going around in circles*.

I took another deep silent breath and said, "I understand that. No problem. Would you like to talk about something else that isn't embarrassing to you and then, maybe, just maybe, you might feel like talking about the embarrassing thing later."

"Where are you based?" the north-eastern caller suddenly asked.

"I'm in our Welford branch, in London."

"London, that's a big place like. Isn't it?"

"Are you from a big place?" I asked, turning the question back on him so that I didn't get involved in a discussion on the geography of London.

"The Tyne. What's your name?" the caller asked.

These two questions, the location of my branch and my first name, are the only questions which we Listeners are permitted to answer under our code of practice. To answer any other questions from a caller is known as self-disclosing and by talking about other subjects it can only complicate things, detracting the caller away from the real topic that they had phoned about in the first place. I have to say though, at that point, I was wondering what the real reason was for this particular bloke's call. I thought that I might know.

"I'm Robert. Would you like to tell me what's troubling you?"

"Are you sure this is confidential. You're not recording me, are you?"

"Your call is totally confidential; we don't record any of the calls that we receive. Neither do we have your number, know who you are, or where you are, so it's okay for you to tell me what it is that is troubling you; only if you want to though." I didn't want to appear to be pushing this guy too much into telling me his problem, so I had now decided to tone it down a bit.

"It would be good if you could record this call. Our call." He lingered over the last two words, which he had uttered in a most affectionate manner.

"Well, as I told you earlier, we definitely do not record calls. So, please feel free to tell me what it is that is troubling you today."

"Well it's embarrassing like. Can you help me?"

My suspicions as to this man's reticence in informing me of the cause of his embarrassment were looking as though they would be justified. I smelt a rat. I have a habit of sighing, sometimes in frustration. Since I had started this job, I had learned how to conceal my sighs. So, I sighed my discreet sigh; I am always patient with the callers, as are all of my colleagues, and I very quietly repeated my earlier assurance.

"As I said, just now, this is a very safe and confidential place for you to share your problems. I am here to give you emotional support and, only if you want to do so, you can tell me what it is that's troubling you, but I can't help unless you feel like talking or want to talk to me." I then became silent.

Silences can be very powerful. I was determined not to speak for one minute. I could hear the caller continue to breathe heavily as he seemed to struggle with his problem. I remained silent, the caller groaned and then, suddenly, after thirty seconds, the caller relented and very sheepishly said, "I can't sleep cos I need a fucking wank. Can you stay on the phone with me? Please can you stay on the phone with me while I have a wank?"

This was what I had been expecting. Experience does help.

"No, I won't be doing that. Is there anything else that is troubling you which you would like to talk about?"

"I just told you. I can't wank properly unless someone is listening on the end of the phone, for fuck's sake, man, stay there while I do it. It won't take long!"

I sensed that this caller was desperate in his needs. He continued his pleading.

"Can you record this, come on, why don't you record this call. Me having a wank and you listening. Come on!"

"Listen to me," I quietly, but firmly, ordered. "You know that we do not listen to people who make requests such as what you are doing now. Do you realise that you are occupying a phone line that is probably needed by a person with a real-life problem? Possibly someone who is suicidal. How does that make you feel?"

"Well, I've got a real-life problem, I'm only asking if you will listen while I have a ..."

I interrupted him. "I will be terminating this call now. Unless there is anything else that is bothering you, I will have to go." I had obviously wasted my breath on him and nothing was going to make him see reason.

The man became agitated; he had probably been here before, on the phone lines, spouting his perverted drivel at whoever was on the other end of a freephone line and who, sadly for him, always frustrated him by denying him his wank.

I knew only too well what would take place next, it happened quite often during this type of call. The caller would become agitated and angry. I prepared to dig myself in for the onslaught that I knew was coming my way and it wasn't long in arriving.

"I need a wank, come on man. Fucking stay there! It won't hurt you. Look, I'll be quick, I promise you. I'll start now. Just stay there, man, I'm fucking desperate! You are supposed to be a Listener. Why can't you listen to me? It's your fucking job, you twat!" he was screaming. "You're a Listener!"

We have to stay calm under all sorts of trials and tribulations and I am always at my coolest whilst being sworn at. I simply replied, "Sorry, but that is not what we do. Thanks for calling. Call back if you have any other problems other than your present one."

The caller's voice rose to a high-pitched squeal, knowing that I was about to cut him off.

"Cunt, you fuck ..." The man's vitriol didn't bother me unduly but no one deserves to be spoken to like that, so I clicked the button and terminated the call.

"Bloody hell," I uttered, mopping my brow with the back of my hand, "what is it with these bloody people?"

It was a fact that all free telephone lines were vulnerable to sexual and other types of predator; it was a massive problem that would only get worse as society deteriorated.

The first thing I did, as the phone went silent, after the potential masturbator had been cut off, was to quickly check that Nicola was still engaged. She was. I really do try not to swear in front of my fellow volunteers, male or female. I had already clicked on the option 'Stop taking calls'; this would keep the phones silent. Now I had to log the call of the sexually frustrated Geordie. Every call received by our organisation is logged, purely for statistical reasons. None of the callers' private details is logged because the Listener never knows who the callers are. Neither do we know where they are, their numbers, or any other private details whatsoever. We are a totally confidential service. But we do log the different types of calls.

I clicked the 'Log Call' tab on my screen and an information box appeared stating the time of the call and how long the call lasted: three minutes and fifty-eight seconds. A list of options then appeared as to the type of call; for example, in need of emotional help, suicide in progress, seeking information regarding joining the Listeners and many others, including the one which I was after, 'Misuse of the Listening Service'. Clicking on this, I recorded it as a 'Sex Call' – and that was it. For a genuine call there would have been a few more boxes to tick.

Nicola had her back to me and was hunched over her desk, deep in conversation with someone who needed her. I took a quick look round the rest of the call centre phone room; the main lights were switched off and only the desk lights provided illumination, as most volunteers preferred that mode of lighting. At night it gives a lovely warm ambience; it was called subdued lighting by my colleagues in the branch. It all seemed so tiny and cramped in this room, which measured four metres by four metres. My work station was situated against the end wall, next to the window that was on my left. To my right was a door which led to a small kitchen, Nicola's desk was slightly behind me facing the wall on my right, so that she had her back to me, and we were separated by a portable soundproof screen. Next to her was another computer station, complete with telephone and a headset that was hanging from a bracket on the wall totally redundant. This was our third station for receiving calls but due to a shortage of volunteers it was never manned, one day, maybe, but not now. We lived in hope but, until that day arrived, there were only ever two volunteers on duty in the Welford branch.

The room was dominated by a large photographic portrait of our founder, a London vicar, taken in 1960 when he had founded our organisation. The reverend stared down on us Listeners in a very serious manner; dressed in his black suit and dog collar he seemed a formidable character. The organisation was originally funded by a large donation from a very wealthy banker in the city of London. The good reverend had wanted to create a safe place where people could call by telephone or in person to share their problems. We only ever took telephone calls here at night but, during daylight hours, the doors were opened for visitors, known to us as face to face callers, who preferred to discuss their problems in person.

At that time, our organisation was receiving almost four million phone calls every year across the eighty branches in Britain. The organisation had expanded over its sixty-year existence. We received a whole host of calls, all made for a variety of different reasons.

The phone system is very sophisticated. All of the calls made by the public travel through the telephone lines to a central computerised exchange and are then distributed onto the next available volunteer's phone. So, when a person decides to dial our distinct free phone number, 333444, that call could be picked up in any one of our branches anywhere in Britain.

I checked on Nicola again; I always checked on my shift buddies, mainly because during the time that it takes to complete our shift together my shift buddy is the most important person in my life. I will support him or her, and he or she will support me through any difficult times during the duration of the shift. The shift which we were working together started at 2am and ran through until 7am; it's the longest and most difficult shift to complete. Lack of sleep was always a factor for me. I am very rarely able to sleep before a shift, it's very difficult for me, although I should be used to shift work after all the time I spent watch-keeping in the Merchant Navy. I usually try going to bed at 8pm and have the alarm set for 11.45pm; sometimes I sleep, but usually not. I find it difficult to sleep during the early evenings as there are so many sounds going on outside, especially in the summer, and I can always hear the neighbour's television or music in my first-floor apartment. Tonight, I had not slept a wink.

Nicola had always been one of my favourite shift partners; she's funny and humorous, of medium height, with long brown hair, a dark complexion and a soft gentle smile that exposed her pearly white teeth. She was, I thought, a stunner but, above all else, she was a very dedicated volunteer. She had thrown herself into the cause, as had all of the other one hundred and twenty volunteers in the Welford branch. She had been in the organisation for five years, two years longer than me. She was one of the very few who went that extra mile in taking on additional duties that would keep the branch running smoothly. She's really good to be with while doing a challenging job like this; I love her – not in the biblical sense, although we frequently flirted – but she was just brilliant to be with. I have a couple of other people who I love to work with but this one, my mate, Nicola, is tops.

I checked my headset, picked up my mouse, clicked on 'Start taking calls' and the phone rang immediately. Breathing my usual deep breath, I clicked on 'Take Call' and said, "Can I help?"

Nothing was said but I could hear a rustling noise and then a click, leaving me with the continuous call-terminated signal. We call it a SNAP call; this is when a caller hangs up without saying a word. These calls happen now and then; maybe because the caller was a female who wanted to speak to another female, a male who wanted a female Listener because he was a pervert, or that caller who had just simply lost their nerve, maybe because someone had walked into the room and disturbed them. I clicked on 'Start taking calls' again and the phone rang.

"Can I help?"

Click, then the continuous tone of a SNAP call. I persevered and tried three more times with the same result and so I decided to give it a rest; I clicked on 'Stop taking calls'.

I looked around once more to see that Nicola had finished her call and was staring over at me. She was wearing a pink blouse and a faded pair of denim jeans. She had worn shoes into the office but had taken them off, as usual, and put on a pair of thick woollen calf-length socks.

I have to say that all through my life I have found most women attractive in their own ways. I have always loved female company for more reasons than one. I have worked with Nicola a dozen times now and it seemed that we had bonded pretty well as volunteers; I found her to be attractive, as well as mysterious, but I knew very little about her and only saw her as a fellow volunteer, Nicola 1880. We never used surnames in the organisation, we were all given numbers; I was Robert 2049, the lower the number the longer that person had served. I didn't really know her but I was able to see a little bit into her Listener's mind. It's the one thing we have in common, as far as I know. She gave me the thumbs-up and I responded likewise. I got up and sat in an armchair which was behind me, allowing me to talk to her and see her without looking or talking through the screen, it's more personal I suppose you could say.

"That was a long call. You okay?" I asked.

Nicola looked pensively towards me. "Yeah, eighty-five minutes, poor woman in her twenties with two young kids, three and five, and her partner has just gone off with her sister's best mate, a girl mate by the way." She smiled mischievously.

"And how's she coping?" I asked with genuine concern. "Not good, I would imagine?"

"No, she was thinking of ending her life and leaving her kids for her mum and dad to bring up. Mum and dad have a load of money. Her partner hasn't disappeared completely and swears he will pay the bills and support her but he loves another, sadly not her. Anyway, I think she'll be alright, it eventually dawned on her what it would do to her little ones if she went missing. I offered her a follow-up call so I'm going to get someone from here to phone her tomorrow, I mean not tomorrow," she said, glancing up at the clock, "later today, at 11am, I'll book it in the diary." She looked at me and said as an afterthought, "Do you know something? Sometimes I hate men."

"Here, steady on, I'm a man."

"I would never hate you!" she said indignantly. "Anyway, you're not a man, you're Robert. How are you doing, mate? Anything juicy to report?"

"Oh God, nothing spectacular and certainly nothing that could be called juicy. I've had nothing but crap, drunks, sex perverts and lost cats. I mean, how can I ever go out and find her cat for her, she reckoned she was in Manchester. I've had loads of SNAPs and a gentleman who wanted me to listen to him while he pleasured himself with his hand, or both hands, he didn't tell me about that bit, regarding his technique. He was totally absorbed in trying to get me to listen to him. He wanted me to record him as well. A totally dedicated, professional wanker."

Nicola raised her hand to her mouth and she was making a noise that sounded like an inflated balloon being released before its open end was tied. "Oh my God, how long did you have to wait for him to finish?" she asked in her saucy way.

I smiled and had a chuckle at that. "About thirty seconds. I terminated him – at least I would have liked to have terminated him for real."

Nicola was resting her hands on the back of her high-backed office chair, kneeling on it looking down at me, when she lowered her chin onto her crossed hands and said, "Oh, it's a shame, isn't it? I wonder why they do that and then call us. Or call us and then do that."

"Cos it's a freephone number, Nic, and cos we are here, that's why they do it. Then again, the guy is obviously ill; I asked him if he had any other issues but it was just the wanking today."

This was now causing me to laugh at how ridiculous it all sounded but, in fact, these 'Sex calls', as the organisation calls them, are a reality and they occur all too regularly in our lives.

"Shame," she said, as she jumped up off her chair, still smiling down at me as she swept by.

"Are you sure you didn't listen to him, Robert?" she said, wagging her finger at me. "Are you sure you didn't listen while he tossed himself off? Want a coffee? Usual, Robert?"

Before I had time to answer she had disappeared into the kitchen, next to the Telephone Room.

Chapter Two

I was staring after her, smiling and shaking my head, not in disbelief but in awe of the fact that she was able to utter these outrageous comments, any time, any place and always sounded totally normal, almost innocent in fact. There was only one Nicola. *Thank God*, I thought.

I looked up at the clock. It was 4.20am, which made me immediately look out of the window. Daylight was well on its way, bringing with it the colourful extravaganza that is known as the sunrise, and, to the east, over the tops of the buildings opposite, I could see the beautiful dawn sky, bright blue in colour tinged with red; it was set to be a gorgeous summer's day. Two-and-a-half hours to go and I was in real need of a meaningful caller. Donning my headset, as would a medieval knight his helmet before going into combat, I clicked the 'Start taking calls' option. As usual the phone rang immediately.

"Can I help?"

A familiar voice replied, a voice with a north-eastern accent, "I canna sleep."

"Oh no!" I gasped under my breath in disbelief. "Déjà vu. How could this happen to me?"

There was a one in ten thousand chance that this call could come through to me, of all people. It was a freak coincidence that this geezer's call could travel through the system and arrive back to my phone line. *Oh well, it's what we do*, I thought.

"Sorry to hear that. Does this happen often? That you can't sleep, I mean," I asked.

"Yeah."

22

"How long have you felt like this, that you cannot sleep?"

"All the fucking time, like."

"Is there anything that will help you sleep? Sleeping pills maybe?"

"No, nothing man, only … well there is something that you could do like. Not pills, but if you could stay on the phone while I …"

I thought, right, that is it, I've had enough, and I spoke very firmly before the amorous Geordie could get to the 'w' word.

"Sir." I almost shouted. "I am going to stop you there. Are you about to ask me to stay on the phone while you masturbate?"

"Mastur … what?" he said, stumbling over the 'm' word. "What do you mean mastur … what's that? I just wanna wank like."

"As I told you earlier, during your original call, it is not why we are here. Not what we do. Please understand this. Now have a lovely day and stop blocking our lines!" I terminated the call, feeling both sad and angry simultaneously. I switched to 'Stop taking calls' and logged yet another misuse of service call.

I really do need a meaningful call, I thought, as Nicola arrived with the coffee.

"You will never believe this, Nic," I said, still not really believing it myself.

She looked at me with great interest. "What's happened?"

"That Geordie bloke, you know, the wanker."

"Yes, the one you listened to," she said, smiling.

"Well I just got him again, unbelievable that he should get through to me again don't you think?"

"He must have really liked you, Robert. Loved you even." She was smiling her largest of grins. "You are a lovely man, Robert. You should be pleased. How long did you have to listen to him this time? I do admire your resilience, Robert, and, as for him, his recovery time is amazing. Don't you think?"

Again, I was left scratching my head in wonderment as to how this girl could leave me speechless. I pleasantly pondered what I would like to do with her and, as I did so, I was admittedly smiling. I always smile when I think of her. I sipped my coffee and gazed out of the window, the High Street below still half dark. This outer borough of the capital could be described as a very prosperous part of London, situated in the area known as the 'Stock Broker Belt'. It was still quiet with the world down below in peaceful tranquillity, as you would expect at 4.30am.

"It won't be long until the whole bloody place erupts into life again," I whispered. It was becoming lighter. It would be completely light in thirty minutes. The orange-coloured street lights gave the High Street a golden aura, even the leaves of the beech trees, which stood either side of the street, seemed to be coated with a golden sheen as they gently fluttered in the soft summer breeze. I much prefer the view at night, particularly now, during the time which I call the silent hours.

The night-time vista is completely opposite to the view in daylight, when the High Street looked not golden but almost grey in appearance. The drab greyish colour of the stone which had been used to construct the buildings in a bygone era was further discoloured and stained by carbon monoxide emissions and the endless years of enduring the extremities of the British climate. These buildings, the backdrop of the scene, always remained the same; it was the activity that changed.

Like a giant ants' nest that is given a tremendous kick, at around 6am every morning the High Street becomes alive with movement; people, vehicles and the hustle and bustle of the population going about their business. The street was generally full of people, together with the high volumes of traffic slowly moving through the High Street and pedestrians trying to avoid the vehicles being navigated by impatient drivers; the game of life was being played out down below. The hectic activity continued usually until about 1am the following day, at which time the frenzied furore began to subside into calmness as Welford slept and we nocturnal creatures, the night workers, can enjoy those precious all too few silent hours.

I have been looking at the view from this window for the past two-and-a-half years, usually once or twice a week. Welford is a branch which tries to, and does for most of the time, remain open twenty-four hours a day, every day, all year round. I have worked all the different shifts of a twenty-four-hour day, so I have observed from the window the spectacle of the performances being acted out below, in the High Street, in all of its differing scenarios and moments of action and, as now, inaction. I liked to think that I used my time at the window in a thoughtful constructive way.

Sometimes, between the calls I have taken, I feel the need to ponder whether I have helped the caller or not. Could I have done anything better? I use these short pauses to clear my head before I get on to the next one, the next caller. I would look from the window regularly as I was taking a call; headset perched on top of my head and my microphone touching my chin, I would usually stare from this window. I get really deeply absorbed in the problems of the caller, listening to the outpourings of their own private worlds; their agonies, their joys, their despairs, their hopes, their disappointments, and their desire to end their lives.

When I look out of the window on these occasions during a call, I notice nothing of the world in the High Street or of the scenes being acted out in front of me. I just listen to the voice of this person, the caller, a person whom I have never met and never would meet, or whose name I would never know, unless they gave it to me, whose location and telephone number is unknown to me. But because this person felt safe here, on this phone line, they entrust me with their life history or maybe a short part. I can see nothing from the window then because I am simply just concentrating so much on what the caller is saying and I really feel that I can absorb the caller's words; by doing this I find that I am able to respond in a more empathetic way.

Listeners cannot give advice and we do not talk about ourselves or disclose any information regarding our own lives.

I always abide by these rules and indeed all of the guidelines taught in the extensive training of which I was once an enthusiastic recipient. I always stick with what I was taught like glue. By adhering to this training and staying with its content, I was confident that I would professionally cope with any of the varied situations that would come before me.

I was still staring out of this bloody window and knew that I needed to get back to the callers.

I can't keep looking out of here, I thought as I started to yawn. The slow gentle movement of the leaves in the nearest beech tree brought me back to reality.

The phones, I thought. The eternally ringing telephones, the lifeline to the many who called our freephone number, and all I wished for now, in the final half of my shift, was a meaningful call.

I crossed the room to turn the air-conditioning down. I'm not a great lover of air con, not in the UK anyway, I would rather have the windows open, but then we were vulnerable to the noise outside in the street so air con it would have to be. Looking around the office, the walls, which were meant to be magnolia, were looking dreary, the magnolia was definitely in need of a touch-up. It was looking tired, like me. The décor was not really a problem though, the magnolia was difficult to see as it was obscured by a couple of large noticeboards showing statistics of call rates and various data for the year to date and the month to date. There were also notices of various types that related to other aspects of the organisation. There was a large number of thank-you cards from various callers who had found out they were talking to the Welford branch when they called. There was also a big board with passport-size photographs of all the volunteers and support staff. All one hundred and twenty of us.

I interrupted my thoughts. Enough of that; I needed to get back to the callers. Nicola sat hunched over her desk, as is her habit when taking calls, her long brown hair obscuring her face as she leant forward.

I checked the clock again before clicking on 'Start taking calls', it was 4.54am; I've never been a clock watcher, the reason for checking the time before taking a call is so that I would know how long I had been speaking with the caller. Simple as that. I had been day dreaming for almost thirty minutes while Nicola was working hard. It was fully daylight now as I mumbled to myself repeatedly, "All I want is a meaningful call. That's all."

Chapter Three

Having clicked 'Start taking calls', the phone rang immediately. I pressed the button on my left earpiece.

"Can I help?"

There was no immediate response, but I could hear breathing at the other end of the phone line. I waited; it's quite common to receive silent calls. I waited a good twenty seconds before I spoke again in a low quiet tone. "Hello, can I help you?"

Still silence, apart from the breathing: slow breathing, not shallow breathing, not heavy laboured breathing, but peaceful breathing.

I waited probably for another thirty seconds. I was thinking how long thirty seconds can seem when you're waiting for someone to speak on the telephone. It could feel like an hour when you're taking a call like this.

"If it's difficult to speak I do understand, don't worry, I'm here for you when you feel able to speak."

I waited and waited, listening to the breathing, and then I thought that I could hear another sound in the background. It was not so much a sound but a harmony that could be described as pleasing, pretty, pleasant and melodic, almost musical. I couldn't immediately think of what the sound could possibly be. It resembled a quiet whistling, maybe twenty warbling whistles or the Peruvian pan pipes all being played at once. I then realised it was the sound of birds singing in the background. Not loudly but the sound could be heard through the phone system, coming across as a gentle muffled sound of birdsong. I then realised that I could actually hear the dawn chorus being played out in the background of wherever this caller's location was situated. I was a silent passive audience, an unwitting listener to one of nature's miracles.

How beautiful was all I could think to describe the wonderful cacophony of sound. The caller's breathing seemed a little stronger and I thought that I could hear a body moving, a noise like rustling bed sheets, a noise we all make when we are in bed trying to sleep, sometimes tossing and turning and other times lying still, moving occasionally, as was this person who I was listening to.

I waited for two more minutes, listening to the birds in the background coming to life and celebrating the new day, as only the natural world does.

I persisted with my vigil before saying, very gently, "I'm here for you. How are you feeling?"

A voice, almost a whisper, maybe a female voice, firstly uttered an unintelligible word but then the caller said, "Hello." A very croaky hello.

It was very difficult to hear the voice.

"Hello," I said, "How are you feeling?"

"I … I am …"

I waited, and after a few seconds asked, "How are you?"

"It's ending now. All ending now …" It was a female voice.

"Can you tell me what it is that's ending?" I spoke very quietly. I always related these delicate scenarios to that Kung Fu guy on the television in the 1970s. Grasshopper he was called, walking across rice paper without tearing it; I always likened these fragile situations to that. I regularly altered my voice to the same sound level as the callers. I try to speak warmly, with empathy, striving to connect with my caller and now, with this caller, I was treading the rice paper deftly but gently, daring not to tear it.

After another short pause, the croaky voice came back to me, answering my question.

"All of it. It's all going to end now. I can't take it. I've had enough, I can't take any more. Ahhh."

This cry of "Ahhh" sounded as though the person on the phone was in despair, as is often the case with these callers. I could hear the breathing, it sounded stronger and I could still hear the birdsong in the background, the orchestra of beauty mixed with this woman's despair.

"I am so, so sorry to hear this. Can you tell me what it is that is going to end?"

"I've had enough of it," the voice croaked. "Enough. I am ending it. I cannot live any more, it's over."

"I am truly sorry to hear this, but I must ask you. Are you telling me that it is your wish to end your life?"

"Yes," she replied. "Yes, I do. I am doing it."

"Would you be able to tell me what has happened to you to make you feel this way?"

"Oh God, it's been years of pain, my back injury." She was a well-spoken lady with a touch of an accent, maybe Welsh. I was so relieved that I had managed to get her talking at last.

"It sounds as though you have suffered a lot. I can understand that. How did the injury happen?"

"Oh God," she sighed. "How did it happen? How did my injury happen?"

"Yes," I answered, almost whispering now. "Would it help you to talk about your injury and how it happened?"

"I suppose it would," she said, her voice seemed to be growing stronger.

"Okay. I am here for you if you would care to talk about it."

She emitted another sigh. It was as if this lady was struggling to summon the strength to start talking to me. I knew that it would take a monumental effort. After a short pause she started to relay her story.

"It was a car accident which caused the injury, it happened thirty-four years ago and I've been in pain ever since. I use crutches or a wheelchair to get about, the pain is always there; it makes no difference what I do, how I sit, whether I lie down or stand up, the pain is always there. Constant throbbing pain that never leaves me alone, always there, always torturing me. Torturing me for my past perhaps."

I was really surprised at how much more fluent and alive this lady had become; the breathing was still heavy but she had really come alive. Alive but obviously in complete despair.

"Do you use painkillers to relieve the pain?" I asked her gently. I could hear her moving as though she was trying to make herself more comfortable.

The caller replied faintly in a strained tone. "I used painkillers in the very beginning but they made me feel lousy in myself and never killed the pain, so I stopped taking the wretched things. Oh, I am sorry to curse to you."

"Please do not worry about that, I may have heard worse," I said this thinking of my earlier experience with my Geordie friend.

"You told me earlier that you wanted to end your life. How …" She interrupted me, stopped me abruptly in mid-sentence.

"I will end it now, today." She said these words in a very positive and determined manner, a firm no-nonsense tone.

"Do you mean that you have made a plan to end your life today?" I asked.

"Yes."

"Do you want to be dead because you cannot stand the pain any more?"

"Yes."

"Have you thought what it would be like to die?"

"Yes, I will be free."

"Free of your pain?"

"Yes."

"I have to ask you. Are you choosing to end your life because you really want to be dead, or is it that ending your life is the only way that you can see to end the unbearable pain that you are feeling all the time?"

"I want to be dead and I want …" she let out a large sigh and stayed silent. I had to ask my next question.

"Did you mean that you really do want to die and, in the process, end the pain as well?"

"Yes, and the rest," she said resignedly, exhaling another deep breath.

"When you say the rest, can I ask what you mean?"

"The other things," she almost shouted. I could sense some frustration in her tone and I was terrified that I wasn't doing very well here. The last thing I wanted to do right then was to make things worse for this lady. A lady who, from the look of things, was about to entrust me with her final thoughts.

"Would you care to tell me about these other things that have brought you to this decision."

I could hear the caller moving again and the chink of glass on glass, maybe a bottle. Then I heard her take a large gulp of a drink before she started to talk again.

"I have cancer also, recently diagnosed at the base of my spine. They think they can treat it and keep me alive for a few more years. I told them no. I asked them, why do you want to keep me alive? I have no life anymore, only this one in my world of pain. There is no life. They have told me they won't do anything without my consent. I can never give them my consent to prolong this hell that is my life. So, I am here now. Talking to you."

All I could feel was genuine pity for this lady. "I am glad that you are talking to me and I am so sorry to hear of your illness. It sounds as though you are not only going through a lot of pain but personal strife as well."

"Yes, it is why I must go now, die I mean. I wouldn't be able to take any more treatment or be pulled about in any way, no, not any more. Death is better."

I felt great sympathy for this woman and I said, "I am so sorry."

She spoke in a tone that was weakened by her illness, a delicate almost feeble tone, yet she was able to admonish me also.

"Don't be sorry. You have apologised to me twice now, there is no need to be sorry."

"Okay." I said quietly, humbly.

"Do you know what death is?" she asked, as a school teacher would ask a pupil.

"What is death?" I asked. I wanted to hear her theory.

She coughed and spluttered gently and it sounded as though she was quietly ejecting sputum from her mouth into a tissue. She recovered herself.

"Death is merely the start of the process of being forgotten."

"Of being forgotten?" I answered. I hadn't expected this explanation.

"Yes, the dead are always forgotten. We are remembered shortly after our demise and then we are very quickly forgotten. We may all think fleetingly of a dear departed person years after their death in a flashback, such as, 'Old so and so used to like doing that, bless him', but generally the dead are forgotten by those who they leave behind. Do you visit graves? Do you visit the graves of your dear departed?" she asked me.

I squirmed in my chair. I couldn't afford to get involved in a discussion regarding her thoughts on death. She answered her own question for me.

"I bet you don't visit the graves of your loved ones, your family. We all do at first, then we forget. The dead are the forgotten."

She made me feel a pang of guilt here. I had not visited my parents' graves for years. She was right, I had forgotten. This woman was having an effect upon me.

"Do you mind being forgotten?" I asked in a mumble. I wasn't comfortable with this conversation. She had stimulated my thoughts.

"Of course, I do not mind being forgotten, my life is over, I will be dead. The dead are always forgotten." She started a fit of coughing.

When she had seemed to recover, I decided to try a different tack. "Can I ask, are you at home?"

"Yes, at home."

"Are you alone?"

"My father is here, we share a cottage, he is ninety-two. He won't get up until ten o'clock when his carer comes. He sleeps a lot." I knew then that I could communicate with this lady.

"I could hear birds singing a short while ago. I can still hear them now in the background as we speak. The dawn chorus."

"Yes, I left the windows open, I'm on the ground floor. It was hot in here earlier and I didn't want the room to smell. The birds are like that in the morning here, well they are everywhere I suppose. Lovely, aren't they?"

"Yes, they are beautiful, truly beautiful," I paused again. I was formulating my next question and, after my pause, I asked, "You said just now that you didn't want the room to smell. I was wondering what smell it is you are concerned about?"

She sighed deeply. "The smell of me when I am dead."

It is always a shock to me when a caller is as blunt as this.

"Are you certain that you will die today?"

"Yes, I have pills, lots of pills."

"The pills, are they with you now in your room?"

"Yes, of course. Where else do you think they would be?"

"Sorry, I was just asking," I said, feeling like a scolded schoolboy.

"That's alright. I know this is difficult for you." She croaked these words in her hoarse voice but I was so glad to hear them.

"I hope you won't mind me asking, but have you taken any pills last night or this morning?"

"Yes, and now I suppose you will tell me off."

"It is your decision to take the pills and I respect your decision; it is definitely not for me to tell you off."

"Yes, thank you."

"Can you tell me what type of pills you took?"

"Yes, they were Diazepam."

"Okay, did you take many?"

"Fourteen perhaps, I don't really know."

"How long ago did you take the Diazepam?"

"Fifty minutes or so, again, I don't really know. It's a lot of pills to take, isn't it?" she asked, almost as though she was seeking confirmation that she had taken enough of the pills to finish herself off.

"Yes, it sounds as though you have taken a significant overdose," I replied almost philosophically.

"That's good," she said.

"I need to ask. Did you phone us because you need an ambulance?"

"No, I could have called one if I wanted one."

"Would you like one now?"

"No, definitely not." She said this again, in a very determined way. I could hear her take another gulp of liquid.

"Are you taking more pills now?" I asked.

"Yes, sleeping pills. I don't want an ambulance, I just wanted … I didn't want … didn't want to …"

"What is it that you didn't want?" I asked her very quietly.

"Not … not to die alone. Not to be alone. I didn't want to die alone. Will you stay with me? Please." She was almost begging me.

This well-spoken lady, who was in so much turmoil living a life that could only be described as hell and not being able to take it any longer, was asking me, a person she had never seen or met, and who she had never heard of before dialling

333444, to stay with her through one of the most emotional and personal times of a human life; its end. She wanted me to stay with her. I always found this amazing. This is how trusting the public are of not only us Listeners but all of the established helplines.

"Yes," I said quietly. "Yes, I will stay with you."

"Until the end?"

"Yes, until the end, if that is what you want."

"Thank you. You are wonderful."

"Thank you for saying that." I knew then, at that moment, that this lady would be dead before this call was terminated.

"Who will find you?" I asked with increasing confidence, knowing that we were now becoming bonded, which enabled me to ask this simple question.

"My father will. We have spoken of this possible outcome, he and I, and I do not want him to find me alive today."

She repeated it again, as if to reassure herself or impress upon me.

"No. I do not wish my father to find me alive today."

Sweet Jesus, I was thinking. *This job is tough sometimes.*

I turned on my swivel chair to my left to look out of the window. I could hear the noises of the early morning below me in the street; sweeper machines, garbage trucks, workmen shouting out to one another. These sounds I could hear but I could not see anything; instead, in my mind, I was focused on a lady in pain, in her bedroom, in a cottage in the countryside, with the birds singing. I was imagining all of this, it being the picture that the caller had painted for me in my mind. "I may be blind but I can see." It was true that we Listeners are blind while taking a call but, if we want to have the vision in our minds, we can see. I treat a lot of calls in this way, apart from a few, such as my earlier one with the Geordie; it was always best not to have a vision in my mind with people like him and, do you know, I never did, but this was different.

"Are you in bed?" I asked.

"Yes."

"How do you think your father will be when he finds you?"

"We have spoken of this. He knows what I am going through, he hates seeing me like this. He may be old but I am still his daughter and he loves me. He will deal with it in his own way. He will give me his blessing."

There was another slurping sound and the rattle of pills as she washed them down with whatever liquid she was using.

"You told me earlier in our conversation that you had your car accident thirty-four years ago. How old were you then? I hope you don't mind me asking."

"No, I was thirty-three then."

"Can you think back to what your life was like then, before your accident?"

"Oh God, yes."

She came to life now as though she had arrived back in her previous life. I could tell that this lady would become stimulated by her memories.

"Yes, it was marvellous. I was a bit of a girl, a party girl, you know, a player. All the men were after me then; I had long blonde hair and they all seemed to fall in love with me. They all said I was beautiful. All of them."

I smiled to myself as she appeared to perk up at these memories. She continued in a most excited manner.

"I travelled all over the world with one of my lovers. We would drink and party all night long and swim in the sea in the morning and have champagne lunches. We never stopped; my mother, dear mother, she used to berate me for it. I was married twice. My first marriage only lasted six months, I couldn't stand it; staying at home all day while my husband dutifully went off to work in order to support his faithful wife, the trouble is I wasn't faithful. I ran off with a brush salesman."

"A brush salesman?" I found myself repeating her words, somewhat surprised.

"Yes, he worked for a company called Clean Easy, he was a bad boy. He had a remarkable sense of humour ... his car registration number was MOP 1," she chuckled, coughed and spluttered all at once.

"My second husband died on me of a heart attack, in a moment of passion, with me; a shock but he was a very passionate man. He always said that I would see him off and he was right. He died on the job."

I could not help but smile here as I felt myself warming tremendously to this most adventurous of ladies.

"I had it all in those early years and I ran through life grabbing big chunks of it and eating it up."

She was becoming quieter at this point, breathing heavier with the exertion of her enthusiasm.

"Then, at thirty-three years old, I died." She almost sobbed then and I could hear her swallowing back the tears.

"Or a part of me, the biggest part of me died," she was wheezing again. "He crashed his sports car. His name was Roger, he was a pilot in the RAF. We had both been drinking and, even whilst driving, we had a bottle of Moet on the go. He was killed and I was only partly killed. I have always wished that I had died with Roger that night. But alas no."

I was expecting tears to come from her again, but nothing happened. There was a long silence.

"How are you feeling?" I asked in my quiet voice. She was breathing harder and I could hear the wheezing of the fluid on her lungs as she said quietly, "Oh, I'm feeling cold now."

I was shaking my head at all of this, and I could hear alarm bells going off inside my head; they were telling me not to get close to this lady, she is a caller and that's it. But I could see much more in her than being just another caller. I have been a great survivor, I have survived a lot, I am tough, I thought to myself. But I am human and, yes, she is affecting me in a way that I do not understand.

"It's probably the symptoms of the overdose that is making you feel so cold. Are you sure this is what you want? I can call for an ambulance from here but you would have to give me your contact details. Is it something that you would like me to do for you?"

"No, this is what I want. I am sorry to put you through this; I didn't want to be alone. You are wonderful." Her voice tapered off and she mumbled. "Truly wonderful."

I felt a lump in the back of my throat, a burning sensation behind my eyes, and I found myself blinking and swallowing before I could reply. I was close to tears.

Shit! I thought, feeling so humble at that moment.

"Thank you for saying that and for telling me of your earlier life and please, don't be sorry, this is what we do, we are here for every one and I am here for you now."

She breathed in as deeply as she could and exhaled. Her words came slowly.

"Have you done this before for someone else, you know someone like me? … Been there for them at the end?"

I would not have answered a question like this normally. I would have delicately parried it with another question back to the caller in order to avoid, at all cost, self-disclosure. On this occasion, however, I decided to be honest and answer the question directly. This lady, in her final moments, deserved me to give to her honesty and frankness.

"Yes, I have in the past, but here and now this is all about you. You are important to me right now. The most important person in my life. I am glad that I am here for you. Honoured."

"Thank you," she replied.

"That's okay," I answered.

"It's funny."

"What's funny?"

"You are the last person I will ever speak with and I don't even know your name."

I was now swallowing back the lump in the back of my throat. I tried to speak.

"My na…" My voice broke, I could not say my name. What's wrong with me? This never happens to me. I was choking, I was close to shedding all of my emotions. I was angrily telling myself 'for Christ's sake sort yourself out, man'. I was truly astounded at my reaction to this woman's story. I cleared my throat and blinked hard.

"I'm sorry about that," I said slowly and sheepishly in my shame of showing weakness.

"My name is Robert. Is there anything that I can call you?"

"My name is Antonia. No one ever called me Antonia, only my mother when she was angry with me, otherwise everyone calls me Tonia, with an "i" in it, if you see what I mean."

"Hello, Tonia."

"Hello, Robert."

"I am feeling colder now and sleepy." She wheezed again, a quiet wheeze.

"I understand, Tonia, I am here for you."

"Until the end? Please, Robert. Until the end."

"Yes, I promise, until the end. Is there anything else that you would care to talk to me about?"

"A final confession you mean? No, not now, Robert, I don't have time."

Tonia said those final words with a sense of resignation. Her breathing was by now much shallower as she whispered, "Your name will be the last word I ever say, Robert." A pause, then she said it again. "Robert."

"I am proud, Tonia. Proud to be with you now, at this time."

"Robert?" she asked.

"Yes, Tonia."

"Do you think badly of me for what I am doing, ending my life like this?"

We are completely non-judgemental so this question was easy for me to answer and, the thing was, I actually also believed in the answer I was about to give.

"No, Tonia, I will never think badly of you. I respect that this is your decision and this is the path that you have chosen. As I said earlier, I am glad that I am here with you. Glad."

"Thank you, Robert." There was a long silence after this.

"I won't be much longer now, Robert." She said these words almost silently. Resigned to her own demise.

"I am here with you, Tonia."

Her breathing had become shallower, a lot of wheezing but still strong, it seemed as though she was lying down. She snorted and it felt as though she had jumped, as if frightened by something, and she uttered in a murmur, "You will stay with me, Robert?"

"Yes, Tonia, I will stay with you until the end."

She exhaled weakly. "Till my final breath, Robert, you promise me, please."

"Yes, Tonia, until your final breath, I promise you."

"Thank you, Robert. I'm frightened."

Shall I ask her for her phone number again to call an ambulance? I thought. *It's too late now anyway.* She had been so adamant throughout our conversation that this was her chosen course, her wish and her right. If I asked again it would probably agitate her when she should be at peace.

"Don't be frightened, Tonia, not now, I am here for you, I am here with you."

"I want to die, Robert," she said in a low whisper.

"I know, Tonia, and I am here for you. I will be here until the end."

"Thank you, Rob ... Robert." She gave another short snort and I could hear her breathing steadily but shallowly.

"I am here Tonia," I was saying. I placed my fingers under my right eye and I could feel the wetness of my tears. She didn't answer this time and I could hear her breathing, still wheezy but audible.

I glanced up at the clock … 6.35am. I had been on the phone to Tonia for about an hour and thirty-five minutes. I swivelled around on my chair and took a glance over towards Nicola. She was staring over at me with a look of concern on her face. She mouthed the words silently, "Are you okay?"

I scribbled on a piece of paper the words *SUICIDE IN PROGRESS* and held it up so she could see. She answered with a silently mouthed, "Okay", and then held up a coffee mug and pointed at me. I shook my head and smiled at her, a shallow, weak smile that probably reflected my sadness. Happiness at that time would have been an aberration, a non-reflection of my true feelings; I had become deeply involved with the caller, Tonia. I turned back to my desk, to her. Her breathing was growing shallower. The wheezing was quieter.

"Tonia," I whispered to her, "I am here for you."

I was thinking to myself as I listened to Tonia take her last breaths. Thinking of how much more difficult it had been to help someone die when you can't see them. I had been present at both of my parents' bedsides when they had passed away and, at that time, I could hear their words and hold their hands. Also, unlike on the end of the phone, I could see their expressions. I could hear their breathing and watch their bodies move with each breath they took but, on the phone, it was not possible to have any of those things. Everything is different on the end of the telephone.

I had always been remote with callers; I had empathy with them but I always stayed remote in my own personal feelings, until now. I knew I had allowed myself to get too close to Tonia but it is what happened today. I had never felt the emotion of my voice breaking before as I listened to anyone. Today, I had allowed this to happen. I could not help it at the time, I had got sucked into a massive amount of emotion. But above all else I was there for her.

"I am here, Tonia. Here for you." I said again, knowing that Tonia was too far gone to respond.

There was no answer, just the sound of faint breathing. I had promised her I would stay with her until the end and I was determined that I would do exactly that.

Time moved on. I looked at the clock above my desk again and it told me that it was 6.42am. I looked around the room. Nicola had disappeared but I could hear voices in the kitchen. The relief shift had arrived and Nicola was probably telling them of the nature of my call. I guessed that they would probably stay out of the way until I had finished; there were indicator lights in the kitchen which shone brightly when a listener's phone line was engaged so they would know when the call had ended.

Tonia's breathing was quiet and peaceful now and I timed myself to speak to her every two minutes.

"Tonia. It's Robert. I'm still here for you, Tonia. Here with you."

She must have still had the phone close to her because I could hear her breathing, maybe she was so far gone that she could no longer hear me. Then, immediately, I thought nonsense. I had been told during my training that a person who was dying was able to hear what was being said until death. I waited, listening to the breathing becoming fainter and fainter.

"I'm here, Tonia. Can you hear me?" There was no response. The digital clock display passed 7am and my vigil continued.

"Tonia, it's Robert. Can you hear me? I'm still here for you."

The breathing was impossible to hear by now and at 7.06am. I could not hear any sound of life, but still I stayed speaking to Tonia. I felt as though I wanted her to speak with me then. As she had earlier, when she had almost come alive with her memories. I was willing her to answer me. Not to die but to come back to me.

"I am here, Tonia." I could still hear the birds, singing as if in a requiem for Tonia. The clock was saying 7.15am when I realised that I could do no more for this caller. Tonia had slipped away, out of her world of pain and torment, and I had kept my vow to her; I had stayed with her until the end.

"Rest in peace, Tonia." I found myself saying. "Bon voyage."

I waited for a few seconds as if I would receive a reply, maybe hoping that she would reply, but the only sound I could hear was that of the birds.

Then I reluctantly pressed the button to terminate the call. All was silent in my world at that moment. The birds had gone. Tonia had gone.

I then suspended business for that shift by clicking on 'Stop taking calls'.

I leaned back in my chair and was wiping my eyes with a tissue as I said to myself, "Well Robert, you bloody well got your meaningful call."

Chapter Four

I sat in silence for a long while, my head bowed down looking at the desk, thinking of the life which had just ended. I felt very alone and I didn't know why. I must have been there for a couple of minutes, thinking of that poor lady Tonia, who had completed her task of escaping from a world that she no longer wished to be a part of. I was satisfied that I had given her all the support that I possibly could have. But it felt strange to be back in the reality of this place. As well as feeling alone, I felt in limbo now that the call, with all of its intensity, had ended. Sportsmen these days have wind-down periods after an intensive contest. I felt in need of something similar, which is why we debrief to our leader at the end of each shift. Tonight, the shift leader was Brenda – but I knew that talking to her would not help me at all.

The door opened and I heard someone walk in. I could hear footsteps approaching me but I couldn't move. I felt a hand rest upon my shoulder and, looking up and around, I saw that it was my shift buddy, Nicola, looking very concerned.

"Why are you still here, Nicola?" I asked. I knew my voice sounded gloomy, but I couldn't help it.

"I thought I would hang on to make sure you're okay. Are you? I was worried about you."

"Yeah, I'm okay thanks. She went and died on me, which is what she wanted. So that's one good thing. At least I did something right." I felt tears welling up again, but I fought to conceal this from Nicola, turning my gaze back down to the desk.

"Robert, you don't sound okay," she said in her quiet husky voice. Her hand was still gripping my shoulder and I could feel her giving me some strength back into my body and my mind.

"Yes, I promise you, I'm great, Nic. It's what we do. I will just log the call and log out of my shift on here. You get off home yourself, Nic, and I will see you soon, I promise."

I felt like giving her a hug but I knew that we can't get that close to colleagues; in stressful situations emotions may grow out of control.

I wish, I thought. I knew she was happily married and I respect not only Nicola but all of my fellow volunteers.

"Okay," she said reluctantly, "don't forget to phone Brenda."

She gave my shoulder another squeeze and walked away. I watched her go and, as she reached the door, she turned to give me a wave, then disappeared from view.

I stayed looking at the empty doorway for a short while, then I turned to my computer station. I logged the call noting that it was a 'Suicide in Progress' in the appropriate place and logged off of my shift.

I got up and took one final look out the window at the hustle and bustle and mayhem going on below in the bright sunlight. The performance that was the normal day was now being acted out down below in the High Street. I walked to the kitchen, where the two morning shift ladies were waiting; they were both very senior experienced Listeners.

"Good morning, ladies," I said in my most upbeat voice and, with a huge, false smile on my face, confirmed, "It's all yours in there."

"Thank you, Robert. How are you feeling?" asked the one called Jean.

"I'm fine, Jean, thanks. The suicide of a lady, it's what she wanted and it's what we do. Yes?"

"Yes, Robert, it's what we do. Go home and get some sleep but don't forget to phone Brenda."

Jean started to walk out towards the Telephone Room, stopped and turned to me and said, "Robert, I have been doing this for a long time. Twenty-six years really is a long time, so I think that I know a little bit about things and the way in which this organisation operates. You did well here this morning. It's a very difficult type of call to deal with. The callers tend to put a lot onto us sometimes. I am glad to hear you say that you are okay but you are probably not feeling okay and you don't look okay, so please remember that you have a lot of support here. If you feel like talking to me, my number is in the branch directory. Please don't be frightened to use it if you feel the need. Alright?" She squeezed my arm as she walked past me.

"Yes, thanks, Jean," I mumbled.

They both disappeared to continue the non-stop cycle of giving a service to our callers. I turned to the phone on the desk in the kitchen and rummaged through the card index to find Brenda's number. Brenda was the leader of the 2am shift and after each shift all Listeners would phone their leader for a debrief, and also to air any problems that they may have taken on board as a result of the calls they had listened to. I had never liked this part of the shift but it is procedure and had to be done. I dialled the number and Brenda answered straight away.

"Is that you, Robert?" Her voice was very posh and straight to the point. Brenda was known as being a very formidable character, more feared than loved in the branch.

"Yes. Hi, Brenda."

"You took a difficult call at the end, so Nicola told me. How are you feeling, Robert?"

"Yeah, I feel okay, Brenda, it was a suicide, she had already overdosed before she called me. She had taken around fourteen Diazepam prior to making the call and she continued taking sleeping pills throughout our conversation. She had recently been diagnosed with cancer in her spine, which was already damaged from a car crash thirty-four years ago, and she has lived in a world of physical and emotional pain ever since. She just couldn't take any more and wanted out. It was, of course, very sad, but I'm fine with it."

I was lying to Brenda then. I was far from alright with it but I wasn't telling anyone my true feelings. All I wanted to do was get out of there and head for home and some rest.

"Is there anything that you will take away with you, Robert, take home with you, after the call?"

"No." I was lying again. "No, I hope you know me by now, I always leave everything behind me in this building. Nothing travels home with me."

"Very good. Is there anything else that you wanted to tell me?"

"No, Brenda. I'm fine, thanks."

"Okay, Robert. Thanks for being there this morning, and if anything does bother you give me a call anytime, I always answer. Bye, Robert."

"Bye, Brenda."

I took yet another sigh of relief and signed myself out of the shift rota at 8.23am. *Shit, I should be home in bed now*, I thought.

I never had a coat, didn't need a coat in this weather, so I let myself out of the kitchen and went down the stairs into the hallway. Standing in front of the big blue painted front door, I took in a deep breath, catching the unique smell of this old building, a smell I found impossible to describe; a smell that hit you as you entered and as you left, not unpleasant but welcoming … a smell that gave you hope.

I opened the door and shuffled out into the street and slammed the door behind me. I took another deep breath and looked up at the sky, which was clear, blue and beautiful. It was always strange coming out into daylight, bearing in mind it was dark when you went in, and all those events, which had taken place within the space of five hours, made five hours seem like a lifetime. One thing was definite, for sure, I will think of Tonia today, especially at around 10am when her father will discover her body. I knew that I shouldn't do so but, shit, I am only human. I was leaning against the door in the now busy High Street when I heard a voice calling my name. I stood up straight and, as I looked to my right, I saw Nicola. My heart skipped a beat and I smiled.

"Robert, are you sure you're alright after taking that call?"

"Yes of course, Nic. I thought that you'd gone home to get some sleep."

"I'm sorry, Robert. I know, as you have told me before, that you are a big old boy and I know that you have been around the block but I don't think that you are alright after that call, and I'm now doing with you what we Listeners do for everyone else. I am being here for you. So, unless you really want to be alone, do you fancy having a coffee before we both go our separate ways?"

I smiled at her, at this girl who was doing what any good shift buddy would do, being there for me. I felt a massive pang of love for her and felt so grateful.

"Yes, thanks, Nicola. I would love to have a coffee before going home."

"Good, well done. Let's go to that place down by the river."

It was only a short walk to the coffee shop and, when we arrived, she picked a table outside while I ordered two cappuccinos and carried them out to where she was sitting. The place had become busy in the early-morning rush. It had turned into a lovely day and I remembered seeing the beauty of the sunrise all those hours earlier.

"Thanks for this, Nicola. You must really want to be heading for home, rather than being here with me. Don't you have to go to work today?"

"No, I have a day off today. What about you. Do you work?"

"No, I'm sort of semi-retired. I tend to work during the winter months. I work in direct sales and I'm well known in the industry. I get loads of job offers when I make myself available. I work to pay off my bar bill."

She laughed at this. "Sounds like a wonderful way of life to me, mate."

"I get by. Are you sure I'm not being a pain in keeping you here? I'm feeling better now, Nic, loads better." I paused, then said thoughtfully, "that's cos you're here I suppose."

"Great, it's a lovely morning, Robert, and I just wanted to be here with you. I'm not really tired yet anyway. Do you live near here?"

"Yes, just over the river," I said, waving my arm in the general direction of my home and almost decapitating a waiter in the process. We both laughed at that and, when we had recovered ourselves, I continued, "I have an apartment there and live with a large temperamental cat called Henry."

"Sounds great. Henry is probably a bit of a character." She was smiling at the thought of me and the cat, I suppose.

She didn't look at all tired. In fact, she looked nothing short of radiant. Her olive skin was emanating health and vitality in the sunlight and her dark brown eyes shone. I was beginning to wonder why we put ourselves through this trauma by becoming Listeners. Why do we volunteer ourselves to suffer the crap that we do? I realised that after taking a call like I just had it was normal to feel the way I do now.

I asked, "What made you become a Listener, Nic?"

She seemed a bit unprepared for that question. She shrugged and then laughed.

"Oh, I just wanted to help, I suppose. Just wanted to do something worthwhile. Then I sort of got hooked on it. The way of life I mean. Why did you join?"

"Well, I had a grandson who committed suicide. He wasn't my real grandson, he was more like my step-grandson. My daughter got married to a bloke who had a son from a previous relationship, and at the age of eighteen the lad hung himself, right out of the blue, no talking to any of us, he just did it. I saw what it did to my family and thought if I could prevent the complete devastation of a family happening to someone else it would be a good thing."

She was looking shocked. "That must have been terrible. What a great reason to become a Listener." She gave a stifled yawn and apologised.

I suggested that we go home. Not together, even though I was by now finding Nicola more and more desirable. It was the qualities which she possessed inside that appealed to me, as well as the fact she looked like a million dollars. We finished our coffee and got up from the table. She squeezed my arm and asked, "Will you be okay now, Robert?"

"Yes, Nic, I will be fine. Don't worry. I will see you next Tuesday back at the ranch, same time."

We were on shift together again next week, and I confirmed, "Tuesday at 2am."

"I'll be there. See you then." She turned to leave with another smile, showing those gleaming white teeth, and disappeared down the High Street into the throng heading for the Tube station. I had to walk the opposite way across the river bridge to my apartment. I suddenly realised I was not tired at all.

Well, I thought, *I won't sleep now. I think I'll go fishing. I'll take my radio and listen to the cricket, catch some carp and sleep in my tent later. I think I might take a few lagers too.*

I started whistling the tune to 'Come Fly With Me' and headed off down the street.

I walked home, stopping on the way at yet another café, one of many on the embankment. This cafe was situated across the other side of the river and I bought a croissant, which I ate alfresco, washed down with a fresh orange juice and a double espresso. The croissant was stuffed with cheese and ham and hit the spot perfectly. I also picked up a filled baguette for later.

I was looking forward to my day by the lake, and all seemed to be at peace in the world.

Part Two

The Road To Damascus

Chapter Five

I arrived at the lake at 11.30am. I thought back to my call with Tonia and the fact that, by now, her father would be up and about to be attended to by his care workers. I imagined him walking into her room and finding her. She had said he would deal with it alright and that they had discussed the possibility of her suicide together in the past. I was really hoping her aged father would be okay and that the birds kept on singing their beautiful mantra, today of all days, in memory of that remarkable woman whose dying moments I had witnessed and which had touched my life. "Death is merely the start of the process of being forgotten," she had said. Wow.

I had loaded my fishing gear into my car and drove to the Fishery, which is a collection of private members' lakes, twenty miles away from my home and deep in the Surrey countryside. There were only a couple of other anglers present on this quiet Thursday morning and it was easy to find a secluded spot on the far side of the lake, where I erected my Bivvy, a one-man open-sided tent; a simple shelter from the rain that I am pretty sure I would not need today but I could sleep in there, on the fold-up bed, if I chose to.

I spent thirty minutes or so setting up my rods onto the pods that held them securely and I was soon ready to start fishing, apart from one thing: I didn't bait the hooks. I merely secured them to the rods so that they were nowhere near the water. I didn't feel like fishing just yet; I was beginning to feel tired. My bed was adjustable and with the back at a suitable angle I was soon sitting up on it, as though

I was lounging on the beach in Benidorm. Only this was so much more peaceful than Benidorm.

I sat back, opened the flask of coffee and was surveying the surroundings looking across the lake in the warm June sunshine. There were bubbles on the surface where the carp were rooting around on the bottom of the lake in their never-ending search for food, and ducks were swimming in and out of the reed banks that were prevalent around the lake's perimeter; I even spotted the blue body of a kingfisher as it flew past me at a very fast speed, low and graceful heading for the far side of the lake in its daredevil dipping flight. I could not have possibly chosen a more idyllic setting on a warm, English summer's day.

I took another deep breath and started to think of my life, wondering if people think I am weird to do the job I do as a Listener. In fact, I think that I am weird in putting myself through the things I do. As I said to Nicola earlier, we are unpaid and today, for the first time, I have brought a call home with me. I had never done that before. By rights, I should phone Brenda now and she would get me some help from the volunteer support team. But I thought, *Sod it, I'll be alright, these thoughts won't stay with me forever*. It was just that Tonia had made such a big impact on me and I didn't really know why.

I leant back in my chair, like some latter-day lord of the manor, sipping coffee and thinking of my life. It was now 2017 and I had just turned fifty-five years old. In my opinion, age is but a number and it is how you feel physically and mentally that dictates age. I felt at that time, despite my tiredness, at least ten years younger than I really was.

I had for the larger part of my life been a very selfish man. I had done more or less what I had wanted to do. How my partner put up with me, during our teens and early twenties, I will never know. My partner's name was Jenny and we have one daughter from our relationship, which had developed early in our lives, a school-kid romance, you could call it. I was just eighteen when my daughter was born; I was so selfish that I named her Roberta after me, the proud father, and my favourite singer of all time, Roberta Flack. I can still remember singing to baby Roberta as I nursed her, the song being, 'The First Time Ever I Saw Your Face'. Jenny has never forgiven me for naming our only child Roberta and she still shows anger about it to this day. I remember going to the nursing home, where Roberta was born on that first day, to look at my little bundle of joy and then I left, heading straight for the Registrar of Births, Deaths and Marriages to register the birth.

"For fuck's sake, Robert," Jenny had said when she had come home with our beautiful little baby, Roberta. "How can you do this? How can you call this beautiful little girl Roberta? Are you fucking mad? How can I tell people she's called Roberta; they will think that we fucking hate her. You are a twat! The trouble with you is you only do what you want to do. You are only eighteen, are you going to storm through the rest of your life taking the things that only you want and never ask anyone for advice or help? Cos if you are, I won't be there and neither will this child. You're a fucking nightmare; you need to think of others, not just yourself!"

I remembered her glaring at me then, as though she wanted to kill me. Her face was red with rage, particles of spittle spraying out of her mouth in her temper, and she said, "But you will never think of others, will you? Never, not a hope that a fucking prick like you will ever care for anyone except yourself."

I remembered it well, only too well, and I had to give credit to Jenny – at the time she was right. I was selfish back then. However, today, I knew that I had been totally unselfish at the time of Tonia's call. Jenny was wrong when she had written me off forever, damning me to a life of total selfishness. Things change. I really hoped that I had changed, but I still wasn't sure.

I lay back on my fishing bed in the sunshine and it suddenly hit me. Tonia had told me that, when she was young, she had rampaged through life, tearing large lumps of it off and devouring it. This was me also. We were both the same. That's where we had a connection. I thought about this for a while before thinking back to my youth.

The long-suffering Jenny never had a look-in at the time and baby Roberta and I ruled the roost. I was an apprentice electrician then, earning very low wages, but I always supplemented this by doing part-time electrical jobs; eventually we made enough money to put down a deposit on a small two-bedroom semi-detached house. Jenny and Roberta and I lived a happy life for two years when, typically, after completing my four-year apprenticeship, I got itchy feet and decided to join the Merchant Navy as an electrical engineering officer for the passenger line Cunard. I waved goodbye to Jenny and Roberta and went off to live the life of Riley, sailing the seven seas on the QE2 and various other luxury ships. I was earning a lot of money and sent large amounts home to Jenny and Roberta. I might be a twat at times, especially in those days, but I always stood by my family. The trouble was I could not keep my dick in my trousers, especially when you were an officer on a cruise ship full of beautiful, unattached women. While I was away at sea, I did have the proverbial 'girl' in every port and, on most cruises, I would always end up in bed with a classy woman or two. I found it very difficult to face poor Jenny when I went home on leave. All I wanted to do then was rest.

In 1982, I was working for the Peninsular and Oriental Steam Navigation Company, aka P&O. While I was serving on the P&O cruise ship, SS Canberra, the Argentines invaded the Falkland Islands. The then Prime Minister, Margaret Thatcher, vowed to liberate the islands and send the Argentines packing. A large naval taskforce was assembled and the SS Canberra was commandeered as a troop ship by the government to carry some of the soldiers who would liberate the islands. The P&O crew were given a choice as to whether or not they wanted to sail with the taskforce. This meant that I could go home to Jenny and Roberta or sail to war. It was no contest, I sailed to war; in fact, I was the first to volunteer. I saw that Britannia required my services and thought that I would finally be doing my bit for queen and country. I was, at that time, a very patriotic young man and actually believed most things that I was told about the United Kingdom of Great Britain and Northern Ireland being a great country.

Two months later, Canberra was anchored in San Carlos Water on the East Falklands with other warships landing with the taskforce, while the Argentine air force, Sky Hawks and Mirages, were flying in on low-level bombing runs trying to kill us all. The Argentine pilots would bomb and strafe us in a determined effort to sink every ship that was assembled there in that anchorage. The bombing continued for the whole of the thirty-six hours the Canberra was anchored there. I found it very strange as I had enjoyed popularity all my life with my peers but here were a bunch of blokes trying to kill me. Yes, actually kill me.

I never understood why the Argies did not go for it and sink the Canberra in that interminable time that the ship was anchored off San Carlos, stuck there helpless. A big fat white target and we would have made a spectacular bang if we had been hit.

Instead, the Argentines went for the escorting warships and I was a helpless spectator as I saw the British ships, HMS Ardent and HMS Antelope, being blown up and sunk. The latter exploding at night in the most spectacular blast that anyone would ever imagine they would see.

I really hated those Argies then. These were spectacular sights, except that in these explosions the lives of British sailors were being terminated, vaporised into nothing in massive explosions and that could so easily have been me, sat there in that very large luxury liner-come-warship. It really hurt me to have witnessed such a spectacle as that and, even thirty odd years later, I regularly feel the pain of it.

These days it is common knowledge that more British servicemen, who served in the Falklands war, have died by their own hand, brought on by Post Traumatic Stress Disorder, compared to any other war. The number of suicides amongst Falklands War veterans exceeds the number that had been killed by those stupid pig shit thick Argentines who had started the whole bloody thing off. It was only the fact that my ship, Canberra, and myself had survived that onslaught that I felt I had been through a miracle and I was determined never to take life for granted again; it probably made me even more selfish and more desperate to enjoy whatever life put in front of me. I saw British ships being sunk and Argentine aircraft being shot out of the sky and I hated war from that moment on.

Great Britain was victorious. Britannia still ruled the waves! Hurrah! I was so looking forward to returning home as the conquering hero. The SS Canberra remained with the taskforce until the end of the war and then the most ridiculous thing occurred; we sailed into the now liberated Port Stanley harbour and loaded up with Argentine prisoners of war, the guys who had been trying to kill anything British only ten days earlier, and took them home to Argentina. I would have made the fuckers swim. The madness of war.

We sailed back home to a massive welcome in the port of Southampton and celebrations were ongoing for a week. Not for me, though. On the return voyage home, I was the recipient of what is known in military circles as a "Dear John" letter. Jenny had written to me and announced that she could not put up with my philandering any more, she had met someone else and was moving in with him in his house in Wimbledon; his name was William.

I smiled here and laughed too, not at the fact that Jenny had left but the fact she had left me for 'William from Wimbledon'. She continued, in her letter, to reassure me that I could see Roberta, now four years old, any time that I wanted and that William was a kind and steady man; not a wanderer like me. She said that William loved them both and could I please send her money to this new bank account, details attached. It was for things for the new house. I thought, fucking hell, now I've got to buy them a bed. I sent them £1,000, the soft sod that I was.

I returned to the small two-bed semi on the outskirts of Welford and walked into a house that was empty; a big leveller for a man used to playing Jack the Lad. Maybe I had received my comeuppance then.

Chapter Six

The years passed. I had become tired of life at sea, so I went to live ashore in 1993 and started a career in sales. To my surprise, William from Wimbledon and I actually got on very well and it is fair to say that William had made Jenny very happy. Roberta was fifteen now. Everyone called her Bobby, much to my unhappiness. Girls shouldn't have boys' names; I had always said that, even though I had named my daughter Roberta.

By the time she was twenty, Roberta was married. We all went to the wedding and I walked my daughter down the aisle. Roberta had married a super guy called Ian, who had a young son called Steve from a previous marriage. Ian was bringing Steve up alone after his partner had run off with a bloke from a group of travellers. Everything went well until Steve, in December 2014, who was then eighteen, committed suicide, completely out of the blue. Totally unexpected. Roberta and Ian, who had two other children by this time, were devastated and it's fair to say I was too. You don't expect to bury an eighteen-year-old. The whole family were numbed by these events and it affected me deeply; me, who had swanned my way through life more or less doing what I wanted to do. I decided it was time to grow up, stand up and be a man. I thought long and hard about what I should do. I had it in my head to do something to prevent other families going through the pain that mine had suffered.

I had heard of the phone-in charities that helped individuals suffering from various types of illness or had problems. I didn't want to work with a charity that helped people who suffered from one particular type of problem. I wanted to be in at the sharp end working on a phone line dealing with a variety of different types of issues, including what we later came to know as 'Suicide in Progress', which is exactly what the organisation did and that is where I headed. I knew very little about them, only that they were on the end of a phone for suicidal people to contact when they were desperate. I attended an information evening in the late winter of 2015 at the local Listeners' branch in Welford.

I was ushered into a large room which had a sign on the door saying 'Training Room'. There were around twenty people in the room who were interested in becoming Listeners and they all sat in chairs arranged in a semi-circle, waiting for the brief lecture to start. In charge of the information evening was a female with a name badge, Julie. She initially introduced us to the Listeners and described what sounded like a rigid training programme, that had to be completed in its entirety, and this could take four months or even more, depending on the commitment level of the trainee.

She then went on to cover what could happen to you as a Listener when taking calls from the public and this is where I noticed that some people were looking rather uncomfort-able. Julie touched on what it would be like to take a call from a person who had taken an overdose and was dying and she described it as though she was that person, even making her voice grow fainter as she went through the process of this imaginary person dying. At this point, we were all offered tea and coffee and I noticed at least six people heading for the exit. Bloody wimps, I thought.

In the second half, Julie continued giving information and after half-an-hour she asked if anyone had any questions. People by nature are sometimes timid, especially in an open forum, and no one put their hands up, except for one. Me. Julie looked over at me and said, "Yes, sir."

"Yes, Julie, my name is Robert and my question is simple. When can I sign up to a training course?"

She grinned at that and replied, "You will have to come to a selection day, Robert, and we will put you through some tests and an interview process to see if you will be suitable to recruit as a Listener."

"Put me down for that please," I said enthusiastically. Everyone in the room was grinning now.

"I like your enthusiasm," she smiled. "The next selection day is in a couple of weeks' time, on Sunday 1st March. It starts here at 9am and will finish at 4pm. A long day, so we suggest that you bring some sandwiches with you. We will provide tea and coffee. That was that. I was hooked on becoming a Listener. The 1st March could not come quick enough.

When the selection day did arrive, it was a typical damp cold winter's day. Nothing would lessen my enthusiasm and the more I thought about it the more I was determined to be selected. I just hoped that I wouldn't blow it. Arriving at the branch, the large blue door was open and standing in the doorway was a very large man who looked a bit like a nightclub bouncer, complete with long black overcoat, woollen beanie hat and broken nose. His name badge said Carl and underneath the one word, 'Listener'. He looked down at me; I am six feet tall and he made me feel like a midget. I introduced myself and was ushered into the training room, where I had attended the information evening. When I opened the door I was hit by a wall of heat and a cacophony of sound. *God, I thought I was the early bird*, I said to myself. It was only just 8.40am but a lot of others had beaten me to it.

I was grabbed by a female whose name badge said Mary and she asked me to fill in a registration form, which was more like an application form. I was then told to circulate around the room and introduce myself to as many people as I could manage before 9.15am and find out if they had any mutual interests; I had to take their names if they did and my chosen interest was fishing, which I had indicated on my form. Years of attending parties on the cruise ships meant that I had learnt the art of circulating very well; however, in those days, I was usually after attractive, unattached women, dressed in my 'whites' or the Red Sea Rig with my electrical engineering officer's gold braid on my epaulettes … I was a very formidable hunter. Here, it was more low-key and I really enjoyed and embraced my task; by 9.15am I had found two fellow anglers and had met many of the people in the room. I was amazed again to notice that eighty percent of them were in their twenties. I felt quite old, but only briefly, when, I suddenly realised, I had seen more of life than they had and I felt that would help me big time. I also noticed there were a lot of the Listeners mixed in with the applicants, easily identified by their name badges.

The branch chairman, a man called Ryan, gave a brief introduction and welcome and then we were split into seven groups of six to work on different tasks.

Each group had two experienced volunteers with clipboards listening to every word the candidates spoke, busy making notes and sometimes throwing in the odd suggestion as they went through the different tasks. In the first task, we were given a scenario regarding a lifesaving drug, but only one dose of this lifesaving drug was available to five people who desperately needed it and would die without it. Our group was handed a file on each person vying for the drug, giving all of their personal details including qualifications, and we were told to pick one person from the five to be the recipient of the lifesaving drug, the other four would die. We were given twenty-five minutes to decide who would live out of the five. I felt comfortable and, quite naturally, I felt that I should take up the role of group leader, the others in the group who were mostly younger seemed to look to me for inspiration. The discussions began and I noticed the two Listeners frantically making notes on their clipboards. At the end of the twenty-five-minute period all the groups were called together and each group leader had the job of explaining their decisions.

This type of activity continued all through the morning until 1pm, when we broke for a thirty-minute lunch break. My head was spinning as I remembered nibbling at my cheese sandwich but, I thought, *so far so good*.

The afternoon session began with a video. The film was of a Listener dealing with a difficult type of call that I later came to know as a 'Suicide in Progress'. I thought at the time this type of scenario was very important to the Listeners because it was mentioned at the information evening and again here now. Is this the greatest challenge I would ever face as a volunteer? I doubted it somehow, not when you are dealing all the time with the unknown, but I knew nothing at that time. The eight-minute video played its course and the selector in charge of this part of the proceedings asked a question. "Can anyone tell me how they would feel about taking a call like that?"

"Satisfied," came a reply.

"Upset," came another.

"I would fight my way through it," said a third.

I stood up, took a deep breath, and started to speak to the room, "My name is Robert and I say this … not to be patronising in any way … but I am older than most in this room and I have seen death, I know about death. I would say that if you have the opportunity to be there with someone who has decided to end their life and by being there you are ensuring that they will not die alone, then that is one of the finest things that any human being can do for a fellow human being."

I sat down and the room went very quiet. I looked up and I could see some of the Listeners nodding their heads; they seemed to be deep in thought at my speech. I fervently believed in those words and because of that I found that it was easy to make that statement. I also thought that this could be the moment that got me selected.

The facilitator asked, "Anyone else?"

A young man in his twenties, a cheeky chappie, stood up and said, "I agree with Robert."

There was a ripple of laughter around the room and the facilitator said, "Okay, let's move on."

During the afternoon, face-to-face interviews were carried out. When my time came, I was ushered into a room fitted out with a series of telephone booths that had phones on desks, each covered with a soundproof hood. They were fitted on a long continuous desk against one wall where there were three work stations and the same against another wall, where there were two. The room was windowless, like some underground bunker. I was to be interviewed by a giant of a man, whose name badge said Jack, and a very petite young girl called Glenis.

"This is the room where we train our volunteers in their telephone skills," said Jack. "My name is Jack and I have been a Listener for twenty years, Robert. How long would you like to be a Listener for?"

That took me by surprise. I hadn't been expecting such an abrupt question. I managed to blag it by saying, "I had a plan that if I was selected, I would dedicate myself to this organisation for at least five years." I noticed that Glenys was taking notes, writing it all down. Jack nodded.

"Good, yes, very good and you are aware that our activities are confidential, in as much as we do not talk about our callers when we finish our shift with our families, friends or anyone ... we are completely confidential. How do you feel about that?"

"Well," I said. "It's confidential. Period."

Jack laughed at this. "What prompted you to apply, Robert?"

I told him of the suicide of my step-grandson Steve and the absolute devastation it had wreaked upon my whole family, and how I had struggled to support my daughter, Steve's step-mum and her husband Ian, who was Steve's dad, not to mention Steve's two siblings, who were obviously my grandchildren.

The interview continued for another thirty minutes before I was ushered back into the training room. It looked as though they were about to end proceedings for the day. Julie, who I now knew to be head of recruitment, stood up and thanked everyone for attending and told us that we would be contacted by letter in the next three days as to whether we had been selected or not.

I thought, *Oh well, that's that. I gave it my best shot. I would be gutted and surprised not to be selected*.

I was walking past Julie on the way out and I turned to her and held out my hand and said, "Thank you, Julie. I will wait to hear from you."

She gave me a big smile, shook my hand and said, "Thanks for attending, Robert." As she continued to shake my hand vigorously, she winked at me and said softly, "We have been very impressed by you."

I walked out into the street and muttered to myself, "For fuck's sake, why can't they tell me now instead of hinting like that. I don't think I can wait until Tuesday, or even Wednesday, it will drive me mad."

As it happened a strange piece of fate awaited me.

I had arrived home thirty minutes later. It was not a long walk really, but a walk that I needed. I grabbed a can of Stella lager from the fridge and sat down, contemplating my day. I thought about the volunteers I had met. They were all so self-confident and considerate of others. They all seemed to stick together as a family. They obviously cared about each other a great deal. What a club to become a member of, I thought. I was debating whether or not to go down my local pub, the Rose and Crown, for a couple of pints with my mates but, just as I had decided to go, I noticed my wallet was missing.

Oh shit, no. Everything is in there, I thought. *Did I take my Viagra out? Yes, I did, it's in the kitchen. Oh, fuck.*

I thought I should retrace my steps. As I was reaching for my coat the phone rang. I grabbed for it.

"Hello."

"Robert, it's Julie from the Listeners."

"Hello, Julie."

"Have you lost anything, Robert?"

"My wallet," I answered immediately. "It must have slipped out of the rear pocket of my jeans. Do you have it there?"

"Yes, it's here, Robert," she replied. "We are still here at the branch, so why don't you pop back and get it. Ring the bell on the front door and I will bring it down for you."

"Yes, yes, thanks, Julie. What a relief," I almost shouted.

"Oh, and Robert," Julie said, almost as an afterthought. "You have been selected. Congratulations. See you in twenty minutes. Cheers."

It took a while to sink in. Then I leapt in the air whooping for joy, grabbed my coat and legged it back to the branch. Julie brought my wallet to me as I waited by the big blue front door and she warmly congratulated me, telling me I was one of only seven to be selected and I should attend the Listeners' initial training session here next Saturday at 10am.

"I'll be there," I said, beaming from ear to ear.

Chapter Seven

The Listener's training course was the most thorough, intensive and comprehensive training I had ever experienced in any walk of life. The trainers covered every possible scenario that we, as Listeners, would encounter, be it on the phone or in a face-to-face interview. The Listeners operated in accordance with a code of practice. From this there were six very simple guidelines and these were mandatory guidelines that we would never stray from.

The guidelines were: (1) Never pre-judge a caller; (2) Never offer advice or your opinions to a caller; (3) Only ever answer two questions about yourself – your Christian name and the location of your branch, town or city; (4) Never offer to meet or contact a caller in any way outside of the branch; (5) Never disclose any information regarding yourself or any other person to a caller; (6) Try to ask open-ended questions, such as, what, how, when, where, and why. These types of questions would always provoke an answer.

This comprehensive training programme was held at weekends and delivered by senior volunteers. The total time the whole process took was 120 hours. Upon completion of this classroom training we were then allocated mentors who would work with us on calls, either face-to-face or by phone. The mentoring would continue for at least eighty hours before we were allowed to take calls and face-to-face interviews on a solo basis; even then the volunteers were classed as probationers, which would continue for three more months and then, if we kept our noses clean, we were finally fully-qualified volunteers.

* * * * *

The lake was shimmering in the late afternoon sunlight. At 5.30pm I realised that I had been sitting here thinking about my life in general for almost five hours. This is not unusual for me; I am a great loner and I am able to lose myself in thought for many hours at a time. And what better place than this? Why had I become so affected by Tonia, who had spent the last two hours of her life with me only this morning. Again I remembered her words, "I stormed through life grabbing big chunks of it and ate it all up."

I realised that was exactly what I had done, the way I had lived my life. I had shown emotion over Tonia because we had both lived our lives in our younger years in the same way, until we hit the bump stops; me with Steve and her with her accident.

Now here, in this beautiful place, I think I finally understood what Tonia had meant by those words, relating to herself and myself storming through life grabbing big chunks of it as you passed through it. I knew that I would always remember this day and the woman I had never met, and never would meet: Tonia.

I was feeling hungry; I had eaten my baguette earlier while looking at the early evening sunshine and this glorious place steeped in a bucolic beauty. I suddenly realised that I had done no fishing at all. My hunger eventually got the better of me and I decided to drive to a nearby village, where there was a fish and chip shop. I returned with a large cod and chips and two pickled onions and made short work of the lot. I washed it down with two cans of lager.

I was sitting in my reclining bed totally replete and very tired at 9pm, with the sun starting to disappear for another day. I was full of food and beer and I leant back on my chair bed, thinking again of the two ladies who had dominated my day. Firstly, Nicola, whose earlier warmness, generosity and understanding had touched my heart. Yes, of course, I was attracted to her in a physical way. She is beautiful inside and out and I think her husband is a very, very lucky man indeed, to be with someone like her. Women like Nicola are a rare luxury and should be loved and cherished. I knew in my heart that I would never have the affections of a woman like that again. I had blown all my chances with my inherent selfishness. "I don't mind being alone," I kept saying to myself in a totally unconvincing manner, "I don't care", which was almost the truth. I didn't think that I could live with another person now, I was too selfish and set in my ways. But, then again, I hadn't met anyone for quite a while. I did like Nicola though and I did think that there was some sort of attraction between us. I decided to wait and see what would develop.

Then I thought of Tonia, the other lady who had touched my heart today and who had achieved the result which she wanted and longed for: to rid herself of the burden that was her life of pain. I was thinking of Tonia and her life and our similarities in character. We were two peas in a pod really, both so bloody selfish, then bang ... something had happened to change our lives and, when that sort of major occurrence happens, we really do change.

I finally said, "Rest in peace, Tonia", followed by, "what a bloody day!" I promptly fell into a well-deserved deep sleep out in the open on a warm and balmy summer's evening.

Part Three

Encounters Of A Different Kind

Chapter Eight

It was the Sunday after the Tonia call and I was working the 10.30am to 2.30pm shift. I was working with 'Big Carl', the guy who looked like a nightclub bouncer. As usual, the phones were busy. There were different types of call on a Sunday, not so many people under the influence of alcohol and drugs but more serious callers. Of course, the big blue door was open for face-to-face callers. If anyone wanted to call in, there is an inner door that is locked and the caller would have to ring the bell. I clicked on 'Start taking calls' and immediately the phone rang.

"Can we help?"

"Ah, yes, you probably can. I need help." It was a deep, authoritative, male voice.

"Would you care to talk about what it is that makes you feel that you need help."

"That's why I am here on this phone call, sir," he snapped in a very stern voice. This guy sounded military and I felt as though he had just put me in my place.

"Okay and I am here for you. My name is Robert."

"Yes, never mind about names! This goes back a long way. I mean, is such an historical occurrence relevant now?"

"Well, if it is bothering you then, yes, I suppose one could say that it is relevant. Don't you think? Or maybe you would rather lock it away in your mind?" I didn't want to push him into talking about something that was difficult for him. He was grumpy enough anyway.

"No, no, I'm here now, it has taken me long enough to get around to phoning you as it is, so, please, let's continue."

"Okay, that's good." I then went silent.

"Well this happened a long time ago, thirty-five years ago to be exact; I was a young man, aged twenty-five. I was a corporal in the army, in the Paras. Have you heard of them, sir?"

"Yes, I have."

"Well, we were sent to the Falkland Islands after the Argentines invaded in 1982."

I shivered at this, as obviously I had been involved, admittedly to a lesser degree than the Paras, but I had been there just the same; we had one thing in common, me and this ex-Para, we could have both ended up dead!

All I could only say to him was, "I understand, please carry on."

"Well, in the Parachute Regiment we are trained to be very aggressive with our enemies and it means that when the shit hits the fan, in circumstances such as the Falkland Islands, then we are the first that Her Majesty's government calls upon."

"Okay, I understand," I replied.

"Well, after we landed in San Carlos Water, on the West Falkland Islands, we, that's Two Paras I mean, were sent to capture a small settlement called Goose Green. This place, Goose Green, had a lot of Argentine soldiers based there, mostly regular troops, such as their Marines, the well-trained bastards." He was in full flow now. "I was a corporal in charge of a section and we attacked in the dark, at night, against a well dug-in opposition who outnumbered us three to one. Have you heard of this battle? Do you know about the Falkland Islands War?" He asked me.

I would have loved to have told him that I was actually there and I knew of this situation very well. But I couldn't do that, so I just said, "It must have been scary."

"Scary, yes sir, it was certainly scary. Anyway, we attacked in the only way we knew how: with maximum aggression. The whole place was lit up with explosions and tracer ammunition, ours and theirs. It was fucking mayhem and very noisy and smoky but we were determined that those Angie bastards were going to get it and we gave it to them hard. Near the end of the fight I was with two others, we had lost contact with the rest of the section, or maybe they were dead, we didn't know at the time. We had just taken an Argentine gun emplacement and were engaging another with a Milan anti-tank missile. The Milan was originally designed to knock out Soviet Union tanks. We put it to other uses and it was just the job for busting trenches, the good old Milan. The enemy never stood a chance against those fucking things. Anyway, we fired a missile at this machine gun emplacement that was shooting at us and it was a direct hit. Boom! The whole emplacement went up in a big explosion and the machine gun stopped firing; then we charged the trench and my mate, Chopper, went down injured and my other mate was killed by machine gun fire from another trench, which we hadn't seen over to our left; fortunately, another section took down that emplacement with a Milan. Tragically, it was too late for my two buddies. I just went ballistic and charged the trench which had been decimated by our Milan missile. I was firing my SLR rifle into the emplacement when a strange thing happened. A young Argentinian soldier walked out of the trench; he seemed to me to be the only person alive. I could see three dead bodies in there with him but he just walked out. I was about to put some rounds into him, the adrenalin was flowing big time and I was intent on destroying anything Argentine at this point, but then I could see that his left arm had been severed just above the elbow and in his right hand he held the remains of his left arm and was holding it out to me, offering it to me, like a bag of fucking sweets, and he was crying for his mama and jabbering in Spanish and thrusting his severed arm at me; all other firing had stopped now. They must have surrendered at that point and I just stood there, in the gloom lit only by various fires that had broken out in their positions, and this kid just walked towards me holding out his arm, shaking like a leaf he was."

The old ex-paratrooper stopped talking and fell silent. I could picture this scene of carnage and this soldier, was relating this story in such detail with such passion. He coughed and I heard him blow his nose.

"I didn't know what to do. We had talked amongst ourselves before the attack and had agreed not to take any prisoners because of the risk of concealed grenades and stuff. So ... so I," he paused again. "I shot him three times in the chest and he fell back into the trench, dead, still holding on to his arm. I knelt down and cried my eyes out until one of our medics came and found me." He fell silent again.

I didn't really know what to say to this man, so I said nothing. We stayed silent like that for a minute or so then, quietly, I asked, "That sounds like a very traumatic experience. How are you bearing up now, all these years later?"

"I still think of it every day and it has proper fucked my life up. I got divorced because of this, my missus couldn't put up with my nightmares and mood swings. I used to have nightmares where the young Argie soldier would appear holding out his severed arm to me, offering me his arm. One night I was so desperate to rid myself of him that I tried to strangle him. I woke up sweating and screaming that I would kill him, only to realise that I had my hands around my wife's neck; it scared the shit out of her and me. She was a wonderful woman, a good and loyal wife, but she couldn't handle that. She left me that day and took our two boys with her. I was devastated and so was she. I tried to get her back but even though I swore that I would never hurt her or the two boys she would not come back and we were divorced. In those days, in the eighties, Post Traumatic Stress Disorder was unheard of. Quite a few guys I served with in the

Falklands have slotted themselves, more fuckers than the Argies killed. Did you know that?"

I answered him honestly. "Yes, I knew that," I said flatly and sadly. "Have you received any counselling recently?"

"No, I ain't ever bothered. It's no use, I just live with it. I got a small job, I'm sixty now, I got a flat and I've got me pension. I do alright but I just had to talk about it today, it was getting to me. I ain't ever told no one of that, you know, the young Argie carrying his own arm, I don't know if I ever will again, but it has helped me to tell you and I thank you very much for listening, sir."

Before I could say anything he had rung off and I was left with a ring tone.

"Fucking hell," I said and sat there thinking of that ex-Para and shaking my head in disbelief. Did I just hear that story or what? He was a typical ex-serviceman, well trained and totally disciplined, and he had obviously just wanted to tell someone of his horrific experience in the Falklands, at the Battle of Goose Green, all those years earlier. He just wanted to get it off his chest. No frills, no additional dramas, just the plain facts. Say it as it was and go. I could only admire the man.

I looked over at Carl and he was busy on the phone, so I logged the call, went to the kitchen, made a coffee and got myself together before going back into the phone room to take another call. I sensed that this morning was going to be busy with good quality calls. I felt happy with my lot. "Bring it on!" I mumbled under my breath. I switched to 'Start taking calls'. The phone rang.

"Can we help?" I said.

A female voice replied, a low, deep, female voice with a London accent. She sounded almost apologetic.

"Oh, err. I was wondering if there was a woman there that I could speak to. I mean, no offence to you, you know, it's just that I would feel more comfortable talking to a woman about what I've done."

"I totally understand that," I replied. "Please, don't worry, I appreciate your honesty. At this moment in time there is no female available in this branch. If you want to speak to a female then I'm afraid that you would have to redial 333444 and hopefully a female will pick up the phone next time, or there might be a female available in that particular branch who you could talk to. But, if you want to speak to me, my name is Robert and I can listen to you and be here for you."

"Oh, I see, uhm, I'm sorry, it's just that it's difficult."

"Yes, I understand how you feel. These things are never easy. All I can say is that I am here for you if you want to talk to me."

"Well, you sound like a nice bloke and it took me ages to get through. I am feeling really low and ... well, cheap."

"I'm really sorry to hear that you feel that way. Do you want to tell me what it is that is making you feel like that?"

"Well, I live with my two kids, two and ten years old they are. Their dad buggered off last year with someone else. Bastard! Sorry to swear." She added her apology hurriedly.

"That's okay," I said, "say it as you feel that will be fine."

"Thanks," she said. "Well, he buggered off, as I said, and doesn't send me any money for the kids and, well, I'm skint like. I can't work cos I'm tied to home cos my youngest is only two. Oh, he is gorgeous." I could feel the warmth oozing out of this caller when she mentioned her kids. A proud mum. "I'm on benefits. Did you say your name is Robert?"

"Yes, I'm Robert. Is there anything I can call you?"

We never asked directly for a caller's name simply because they might not want to reveal their real name. But they might be happy to use another name. I was thinking that this lady would give me her real name.

"Yeah, I'm Jane."

"Thanks, Jane. You were saying that you are receiving benefits."

"Yeah, I'm on benefits, I've always been on benefits. My mum, she's still on benefits, she always has been. I'm twenty-six years old with a ten-year-old kid. Pregnant at sixteen I got a flat from the council and money to live on. Course I'm on benefits. I don't know how to work. I would like a proper job but I don't know how to work and I ain't working in that bloody chicken factory or anything like that. See what I mean, Roger?"

"I'm Robert and, yes, I understand what you are saying, Jane, completely, and I admire your honesty, if you don't mind me saying."

I knew that for many years, society – and when I say society I mean successive UK governments – had created generations of a new class of person who were totally reliant on benefits. They were either incapable of working or did not have the desire to work. Some would say they were lazy and should be forced to work, but the reality is that for these people the benefits system had become a way of life. It was common for young girls like Jane to become pregnant at sixteen or younger and then be given a flat or a house and money, public money, to live on and the more children they produced the more public money they received. It seemed crazy but it was true. This was the system that the present Tory government wanted to change in order to save money and they had introduced vicious cutbacks and austerity; people on benefits were an easy target and the fat cat Tories didn't give a shit about the people affected.

I continued my conversation with this caller.

"Can I ask, Jane, is there a problem with your benefits?"

"Yes, what a bloody fiasco. It's because they are in the process of changing the system to Universal Credit now and, while they are doing that, they're messing up the old system and the upshot is that, quite honestly, I'm not getting any money through."

"Have they, the benefits people, given you any explanation as to why this is happening, Jane?"

"Not a dicky bird. They are useless, they keep saying it will be sorted out soon and I've been waiting nine weeks and nothing has happened. They must owe me over two thousand quid. I'm scared to count it up. I can't pay the rent and the landlord is threatening to evict me. I can't even buy food."

I had, in the recent past, received calls from some very desperate, sometimes suicidal, people concerning this subject. I detested politicians. In my experience, most politicians are quite wealthy and the decisions they make never affects them because they are protected by their wealth. It is a fact that the bungling incompetence of politicians only affects the worst off, the poor. I think that these so-called politicians are nothing other than a gang of self-serving morons with oversized egos. I really believe that the incompetence of the current bunch is far worse than this poor old country has ever had to suffer before. Of course, as a Listening Volunteer I know I must keep my thoughts to myself.

"Have you thought of going to the Citizens Advice Bureau, Jane?"

"Oh, Roger, mate, I ain't phoning about help with getting the money," she said with a sigh. "Do you remember how I said I felt earlier?"

"Yes," I said, glancing at my notes, simultaneously mentally forgiving her for getting my name wrong again. It didn't really matter what she called me; it was her I was interested in.

"You said you felt low and cheap."

"Well, I do and I will do anything to protect my kids. Like a lioness with her cubs, my mum says I am. So I did something to get the money to feed my kids."

"Okay, I understand. Do you feel like talking about what you did, Jane?"

"Yes, Roger, I will come to that, but I am so ashamed, so fucking ashamed."

She broke down into tearful sobbing. She was crying her eyes out and there was nothing I could do but listen. It was the deepest sobbing that I had ever heard, God only knew what had happened to this poor woman. It took her more than five minutes to regain her composure. I was trying to offer words of comfort and support. I found these situations difficult; I wasn't doing very well. I was saying things like, "Don't worry, it is best to let your emotions out", and "There is plenty of time, Jane, just get yourself feeling comfortable before you start again. Okay?"

What else could anyone say? I knew that I needed to stop being so self-critical.

"I'll just go and get a handkerchief a minute," she said, still sobbing. "This one is all wet."

"That's okay, Jane, no problem, I ain't going nowhere." I could hear her fumbling around with items in a drawer or cupboard. Then I heard her blow her nose.

"Oh, wow," she said. "I'm so sorry about that."

"Jane, that's okay, really it is. It is best to let your emotions out sometimes rather than keep them bottled-up. Don't you think?"

"Yeah, mate. Thanks, Roger, I feel a bit better now. I don't know what happened then."

"It sounds as though you have been through a lot, Jane; the break-up of your relationship, the mess up with your benefits and looking after your children, it's a lot to have to deal with. You are bound to feel low some times. Don't you think?"

"Yeah, that's right," she sniffed.

"You were telling me that you would do anything to protect your kids, like a lioness with her cubs, your mum says."

"Yeah, that's it, Roger, I am like that. I love them so much and they don't deserve all of this, what with their dad and everything; they are with my mum now, she looked after them last night, she is brilliant with them. Anyway, I was telling you I was in arrears with the rent and everything and, well, I did something that I am finding hard to come to terms with."

"You don't have to tell me anything, Jane, if it's difficult for you. We can just chat here for a while, it's okay." I wanted to put her at ease but I was also very curious by now. What had happened?

"No, mate, I phoned here to confess my sins so I will. I've got a friend, she's got two boys, thirteen and eleven. She's on her own like me and, well, she struggles with money. I mean at their age her two boys want everything they see; designer clothes, all the gadgets, computers and everything. Well, my mate, she's in her early thirties, a bit older than me, I'm twenty-six. I tell you mate, we slap up well. Know what I mean? If we go out for a drink all the blokes are after us. Older blokes with loads of money and the younger ones with their big biceps and tattoos with their brains in their trousers. They're all chasing after us. It's got so bad we don't bother going out any more, we stay in with a few bottles of fizzy wine and a take-away meal. All those blokes are tossers, just after one thing, and it's not intelligent conversation cos most of the twats are thick as shit." She spat those words out with pure contempt.

This conversation was now becoming easy for me. Jane had opened up and was really letting it flow.

"So, cutting to the chase, my mate, her name is Annie, she has got a part-time job, with a firm down the West End. She … err … well she goes out with men that they put her in touch with. Do you understand where I'm coming from, Roger?"

"Yes, I think I do. Are you saying that Annie works as an escort, Jane?"

"Yes, that's it in one, mate. She gets paid three hundred pounds a night by the agency and she keeps anything else she earns, any extras, if you see where I'm coming from?"

"Yes, I understand."

"So, last night, I did it too."

"When you say you did it too, do you mean that you worked as an escort?"

"Yeah, that's what I did, for the money, I prostituted myself."

"And how are you feeling now, Jane?"

"Well, you just heard me, Roger, I'm proper fucked-up." She laughed at her own words. "You could say in more ways than one. Do you know what I mean? But I am eight hundred quid the richer and if I had stayed with him all night I could have been over a grand better off, which would have sorted my problems out."

"I hope that you don't mind me asking a question, Jane."

"No, no, after what I was up to last night, I can answer any question from you, mate."

"Are you hurt in any way physically, Jane?"

"No, not hurt physically just, well, just in my brain, in my mind like." I could hear her blow her nose into the tissue again. "I didn't get tied up or anything. It was, well, it was normal like. I went down on him and ...." I interrupted her.

"That's alright, Jane, you don't have to go into the details, I err … get the gist." I was blushing a little.

"Yes, sorry, mate. I must sound like a right old tart. Anyway, I came back home after I left him and I got in the bath and scrubbed myself, you know, down there, I scrubbed and scrubbed trying to wash him out of me; even though he used a condom I felt dirty. I had to, well, I had to wash him away from me, which I did, but the memory is still there gnawing at me, at my mind."

Jane's pain was coming across to me. I could feel her mental anguish.

"Would you say that it has left a mental scar on you, Jane?" I asked her.

"Yes, probably. Annie says that it's perfectly normal to feel like I do and I should think of the money and the kids and she reckons that the more I do this the easier it will get. She says that she enjoys it now."

"Is it something that you think you could enjoy, Jane?"

"Dunno, mate. I can see where Annie is coming from. If you get the right bloke you can have a great time and he, him last night, was a perfect gentleman; about forty, an Arab bloke, he appeared to be well minted, you know, wealthy, and he wants to see me again on Wednesday. It will be good for a grand and my money worries will disappear, and when those tossers in the government pay up then I will be quids in. Won't I?"

"Will you see him again on Wednesday, Jane?"

"Annie tells me I should. Trouble is she's doing it once a week now, I think she's hooked on it, sort of relying on the money to get by on. She spends it all on her boys, apart from some bits and pieces for her; new dresses, a bit of jewellery, good perfume and stuff that she needs to wear for the … for the job."

"Do you think you really will see him again on Wednesday, Jane?" I asked again.

"I don't know, Roger, is the truth, I really don't know. He was okay with me, I didn't have to do much, he took what he wanted from me and that was it. But, as I said, I feel low and cheap."

"Yes, I understand. How do you feel in yourself now that you have told someone other than Annie?"

"Oh, better I suppose, I don't know really. I don't feel as ashamed as I did earlier."

"I'm glad about that. And do you feel depressed about it? You certainly let your emotions out earlier."

"I don't feel depressed. I don't know how I feel. Ha, I know what you're getting at. You lot, Listeners, Samaritans or whatever, are obsessed with suicide, ain't ya? Annie told me that. She's phoned you. Anyway, Roger I ain't doing that mate, I got my kids."

"I'm glad that you don't feel that way, Jane."

"Yes, I need to be with my children and take care of them as well as I can. It's what they deserve and I will do whatever it takes to give them a good life, as they should have. You know, Roger, it ain't as though I'm a virgin, is it? Far from it, mate. You know what I mean?" She was sounding more upbeat now. It appeared to me that Jane was a very resilient character.

"I fully understand Jane," was all I could say to that statement.

"Listen, Roger, it has been good to speak with you and thank you very much for listening to me going on about all this shit, but I got to pick the kids up now, and I can't be late for mum as she goes to her church. Perhaps I should go with her, aye? Say a quick prayer to him upstairs begging for forgiveness. Know what I mean?" Although Jane now sounded much happier, I couldn't help but wonder whether or not it was a mask to her true feelings.

"That's okay, Jane. If you are feeling low again please phone us, we are always here for you."

"Yeah, Roger, I will. Bye."

I clicked on 'Stop taking calls'. That was it, I was thinking we get so deeply involved one minute with the caller's troubles then the next minute they're gone. I would forgive her for calling me Roger. I turned to stare out of the window. I had taken two calls today and both callers had said their piece and then abruptly disappeared. I knew that we were not there to heal them but sometimes it was hard when they left me.

What a twat I am, I thought.

I looked over to see where Carl was and I could hear the giant of a bloke crashing around in the kitchen. I checked my mobile phone, which was on the desk beside me, on silent of course. I had heard it vibrate during my call with Jane; there was a text from a number that I did not recognise. Christ, it was from Nicola. I was gobsmacked. I never even had her number logged into my phone – there was no need to keep any volunteer's numbers as they were all available on the branch directory. Everyone working in the Welford Branch was in the directory and all of their numbers were available to any volunteer.

She was asking how I was feeling after Thursday morning, with the suicide caller, and would I care for a drink after my shift in the pub called The Duck over the road. *What could be the matter?* I thought. I had never received a private message from any Listener before, let alone her. She ended her message with a solitary 'x'. I texted back in the affirmative and would have to wait until the end of my shift to see what it was all about.

I had made a start in logging the call I had taken with Jane and was thinking about how, in 2017, in Britain, a young mum has to go out and prostitute herself because the government totally cocked up her benefit payments. A massively wealthy country with a shit government which doesn't give a damn about ordinary people. How can this happen? It's crazy.

I knew that Jane would be seeing her Arab gentleman on Wednesday, of course she would. Supply and demand; she had something to sell and the Arab, by the sounds of it, had the money to pay for it. The trouble is Jane, like her friend Annie, would become used to having the money to spend on her kids and she would get sucked into the spiral of the game of prostitution. That could work out well – or it could be her downfall.

Chapter Nine

The morning's calls had been good ones so far and, in spite of my feeling earlier that they had ended somewhat abruptly, I felt a warm glow, a good feeling. I smiled and thought that maybe my halo had slipped. I wandered out to the kitchen to see Carl, only to find him sprawled out in an office chair.

"You alright, Carl?" I asked.

"What, oh yeah, Robert, I'm fine mate. Heavy night last night and I really don't feel like doing this today. Listening to all these fucking people, mate."

I was a bit taken aback to hear this from one of the mainstays of the branch. It wasn't the first time that anyone had confessed to me that they were not in the mood for completing their shift. We are, after all, only human and we all get problems but Carl had put a lot of feeling into that statement. I started to make myself a coffee.

"Would you care for a coffee, Carl?"

"No, I'm cool, mate, thanks. I don't mean to sound negative; I've been doing this a little bit longer than you, three years plus a bit more, and it's the first time I've felt this way. We still got an hour-and-a-half to go and it's driving me mad."

"Okay," I said. *What the hell was happening to all my fellow Listeners*, I thought. Nicola's strange message, Carl appearing to lose it and me nearly losing it the other morning over Tonia.

"You sound so fed-up, Carl," I said, trying not to sound like I would be with a caller.

"Yeah, mate, girl problems."

Carl was in his early thirties and at six feet ten inches tall he was like a beacon for the girls. He played Rugby for the local club and was one of the borough's characters.

"Sorry to hear that, mate," I said. "Girls can always fuck with your head. Why don't you just chill out in here or go sit in one of the armchairs next door and sod the calls for the rest of the day. Or, if you want to go home, I can call the leader and say that you have been taken ill and we can close the branch. What do you think?"

"Yes, Robert, thanks. I will sit in there," he pointed to the phone room. "I'll hang out in there till we finish, if that's alright with you. I think we should keep the branch open."

"No problems, Carl. If you want to talk … well I'm here, mate."

"Yes, thanks, Robert, I appreciate that, it's just that I'm tired. I think I might take a sabbatical for a few months." I nodded in agreement.

Everyone has their stress levels. Listeners in particular could be vulnerable to massively stressful forces. We did have to listen to some pretty harrowing stuff. Sabbaticals were available to anyone who felt that way or just felt like taking a break from duty for a while. All Carl would have to do was arrange it with the branch chairman, Ryan.

Out of the blue, a very loud bell rang, which made us both look up with a start. Ding Dong. It was the door bell, which could only mean one thing – we had a face-to-face caller wanting to see someone.

"Oh no," said Carl. "Shit."

"Don't worry, mate, I will take it," I said as I looked up at the CCTV screen and saw a young woman with long black hair waiting by the inner front door. I made a grab for one of the emergency alarm buttons which we had to wear when dealing with a face-to-face caller.

"You going to be okay, Carl?" I asked as I headed for the door. Carl gave a thumbs-up. Even that looked hard work for him.

I headed down the stairs towards the front door. As with all things in this place, there is a set procedure for dealing with face-to-face callers, hammered into us in training, and I always religiously stuck to my training, one hundred percent, or so I thought.

I opened the door and I was confronted by a petite lady, in her twenties maybe. She was of Chinese appearance, I think, Asian anyway. I gave her a big smile and greeted her with a "Hi". She looked up at me and gave me a nervous smile.

"Are you a Listener?"

"Yes, I'm a Listener. My name is Robert." I held out my hand.

She took my hand in her own very small hand and said, "I'm Jade. I thought you people would wear a black suit and a tie. Sorry, I did not know what to expect, maybe I expect a religious man like priest or monk. But you look so relaxed."

Her accent was Asian, maybe Chinese, and she missed certain words out of her vocabulary; you couldn't call it pidgin English but it definitely wasn't perfect. She was still pretty easy to understand though. I was feeling a little bit taken aback by her thinking I may be some sort of holy man. I looked at myself up and down, I was wearing denim jeans with a pair of trainers and a white short-sleeved shirt. Not much like your average vicar.

"Oh Jade, erm, we're relaxed here and we're not a religious organisation. If that is what you wanted you won't find it here."

"Sorry, no. I wasn't looking for a religious thing or a holy man. It is just my thoughts, that's all. You are lovely, please, you will do."

I was now smiling, glad that "I will do". She did have a lovely voice with the inevitable Chinese influence in her words, which came out in a very light singsong sort of way.

"Would you care to come in, Jade?" I asked, waving towards the stairs.

She looked up at me with uncertainty and finally said, "Yes, okay, thank you." She stepped inside.

I pulled the outer door, the big blue door, shut; we could not accommodate another caller now. I pulled the inner door shut; security was paramount in the branch. I took her up one flight of stairs to another door with a keypad lock on it, into which I punched the current code number, 7840, and gained entry. We entered into another lobby with three doors facing us. On the right was the kitchen, which led to the phone room. Only qualified Listeners could enter here and the door was protected by another keypad lock. The centre door was a toilet, and the left-hand door was the face-to-face meeting room. I opened this door for her and switched on the lights, although they were not really required as it was another perfect summer's day, and I ushered her into the meeting room. The room was small with two armchairs facing each other and a coffee table in the middle. The table had a telephone on it and a box of tissues; apart from these three pieces of furniture it was empty. I pointed Jade to the furthest armchair, a comfortable chair with wooden legs and wooden arms.

I smiled at Jade and asked, "Would you care for a cup of tea or coffee, Jade?"

"Ah, yes please. Do you have green tea?"

"Yes, we have."

"That would be good, thank you," she said with a beaming smile.

"Okay, give me a few minutes, just relax in here."

I went out and punched in the code on the kitchen door lock and walked into the kitchen. I filled the kettle, switched it on and then went across to the desk with the phone on it. I dialled the leader's number. This morning it was Bryn, the patriotic Welshman, a former coal miner from the Rhondda Valley.

"Hello," Bryn answered, almost immediately.

"Hi, Bryn, it's Robert at the branch. Just wanted to let you know I'm doing a face-to-face call now."

The deep Welsh voice answered. "Okay, Butt. Bryn always called me Butt. He really was annoying. "Make sure the outer door is shut, will you?"

"That's done, Bryn."

"That's great then. Butt, let me know how it goes. Good luck," he said and hung up. He was obviously busy with something at home and wanted shot of me. I looked into the phone room and Carl was slumped in one of the armchairs.

"Are you alright, Carl?"

"Yeah, mate. I will phone you in twenty minutes."

The shift buddy of a volunteer conducting a face-to-face interview always phoned twenty minutes into the interview for security reasons, or to give the Listener a get-out clause if it was needed.

"Cheers, Carl. Chin up, mate."

I went back out into the kitchen, made myself a cup of coffee and a green tea for my caller and went back into the face-to-face room. Jade was sitting there as quiet as a lamb.

"Sorry, it took a little longer than I thought," I said, placing the green tea on the coffee table in front of her.

"It's okay," she said in her singsong voice. For the first time I was able to properly look at Jade. She was, at a guess, approximately five feet two inches tall, petite, wearing a white long-sleeve blouse, a tight pair of faded denim jeans and sandals on her bare feet. She had long brown hair and she was very attractive; her face was like the most fragile porcelain, her skin seemed to be stretched across it tightly, but not unpleasantly, and this made her fine far eastern bone structure more prominent. I subconsciously decided that she was not just attractive but damned right beautiful. I noticed a gold chain around her neck with a large green stone, hanging in her open-necked blouse. She looked at me and then up to the ceiling to the camera that was fixed there.

"Am I being filmed?" she asked.

"No, Jade, that camera is pointed at me and definitely not at you. It is there purely for my own security."

"Okay, as long as I am not in the film."

"No, you're not, I promise."

"Before you ask, I come from Vietnam. Ho Chi Min City, do you know it?"

"I have heard of it. Did it used to be called Saigon?" I always avoided getting involved in answering any questions from the callers like this and always gave vague answers and, if possible, asked the caller a question.

"Yes, it was Saigon until the end of the American war. I have been here ten years. I come to university first and now I live here. I have British passport," she said the last words very defensively, as though she was afraid I might have her deported. "I have worked here and I pay tax to British government. I don't mind to pay tax to government."

"Are you working now, Jade?" I asked. I was trying to get her to open up so she was able to tell me the real reason she was here.

"Yes, I am a computer technician. I know a lot about these things and work for Barclays Bank. I am what you call a software analyst."

"Wow, that sounds good. What prompted you to ring our bell today?"

"Ah, this is difficult. I don't think you can help me but I needed to talk to someone."

"Well, I am here for you, Jade, and you can air your emotions here with me and it is completely confidential. I don't know who you are, only that you are Jade originally from Vietnam. That's it. I don't need to know any more private details from you unless you wish to tell me. Perhaps you can tell me how you are feeling."

"Yeah, I'm not very good at the moment, obviously not or I wouldn't be here in this place." She laughed at this and I smiled with her.

"Can you tell me why you are not feeling too good at the moment?"

"I am being controlled."

"When you say that you are being controlled, do you mean by a partner?" I asked her quietly and calmly, trying to convey my interest to her.

"Yes, that is exactly what I mean. Have you had this sort of problem before?"

"We see a lot of people, Jade."

"Yes, I can imagine." She was sitting upright, her dark eyes seemed to pierce mine. I thought, *This woman is strong, very strong*.

"Do you want to tell me about your partner?"

"He is cruel, he is a violent bully, he is a drug dealer, he is sadistic and he should be in prison."

I was listening to this intently and I could detect the venom in her tone. I was wishing I could make notes, which is not possible in a face-to-face meeting, unlike on the phones, where note-taking is common practice, although any notes taken regarding any caller were always shredded at the end of the shift. I listed the points that Jade had just made about her partner back to her.

"Jade, you have just told me that your partner is cruel, he is a violent bully, he is a drug dealer, he is sadistic and he should be in prison. Is that right?"

"Yes, that is correct." The way she answered me was similar to an automated reply, immediate and devoid of feeling.

"This man is your partner and everything that you have just told me about him sounds to me very bad, do you realise that?"

"Yes, I am sorry." She said, looking down at the floor as though she were ashamed. "This is the truth about him, that man." She spat these words out. I was watching her face, full of anger.

"Please do not be sorry, Jade, say what you think. Do you live with this man?"

"I do, yes."

"Can I ask you, Jade. Do you love this man?"

"Yes, I suppose so. Now you will ask how is it possible that I can love a man like this?"

"No, I wasn't going to ask that simply because it is none of my business. I was going to ask you, what do you want?"

"What do I want?" she repeated back at me, a look of bewilderment on her face. "I want to be free."

"Free of your partner?"

"Yes." She said it almost in a whisper, lowering her head once more and staring at the floor.

"Then I must ask you. Why don't you leave?"

"Because he will kill me if I leave him. He really will." Jade repeated those words with great emphasis. "He really will."

She was looking at me now, her beautiful face showing some signs of strain. I could detect despair, if not fear, in her voice – or maybe a mixture of both.

"Have you tried to leave him in the past?"

"Yes, and he caught me and beat me like a dog. He is a drug dealer; I know a lot about his business and what he does. If anyone crosses him, he has them dealt with." She went silent and looked down at the floor once more.

"Jade, when you say dealt with, can you tell me what it is that you mean?"

"Beaten up. Not killed. But that will come, believe me, that will come, one day he will cause death; the death of his enemies, of which there are many, and my death, he will kill me, I know it. He is in his ascendancy, on the way up, the more money he makes the wilder he is. He calls me his little Chink. He loves me, or should I say he loves the way I look; he is addicted to me."

She held out her hands with her palms facing inwards and she moved them slowly up and down her body, almost touching her breasts in a slow seductive manner, as would a dancer drawing attention to the way she looked.

"Do you understand?" she asked.

I was looking at the floor now.

"Yes, I understand," I said very quietly. I felt as though I was losing control of the interview and I had become embarrassed, unable to look Jade in the eye and uncertain what to say next. She had really disconcerted me.

"Can I ask, what is the green stone you are wearing?" I asked this question in an attempt to move the conversation on, but realised immediately that I had drawn attention to her body again. *Idiot*, I thought.

"This," she said, taking hold of the green stone in her small hands. "This is my only true possession, the only thing in the world that is mine. It is a Jade stone."

The intercom phone rang. I looked at my watch. I had been with Jade for twenty-five minutes.

"Excuse me, Jade." I picked up the phone and Carl's voice boomed out "Are you alright, mate?"

"Yes, thanks, everything good," I answered and hung up. She still held the stone in her hand.

"Is there anything of significance about a Jade stone? Does it have a meaning?"

"Ha," answered Jade. "The philosopher Confucius said … 'Jade is like virtue and it's brightness represents heaven'." She looked down again.

"It is very beautiful," I said. "Both the stone and the explanation by Confucius. Was it a gift from someone?"

"My grandmother gave me this," she said, still holding the jade stone. "Before I left home. It is the only thing I own other than money, which is in my account. I am not very virtuous now, though, am I?" Jade sighed.

"What do you want to do, Jade?"

"The only escape I have now is death."

"Have you thought about ending your own life?" I asked.

"Yes, of course."

"When was the last time you felt that way?"

"Now." I could see the tears in her eyes.

"How do you propose to end your life," I almost whispered.

"Various ways."

"Is it the only way you can see to escape your partner?"

"Yes, probably. Oh, I don't know anything any more. I am so sorry; I should not have come here today. It's not fair, not on you or anyone. I can go back to Vietnam but he will follow me and my family are there and I don't want them involved. I don't want them hurt." She became silent and was breathing heavily, still clutching the stone.

"You said earlier that you loved him. Is that the reason you are unable to leave?"

"Yes, that is it. Isn't it? I do love him." It was as if I had answered the question for her.

"You also said earlier that he was addicted to you. Are you addicted to him?"

"Oh, Robert. That is very clever. Yes, very clever indeed. I hadn't thought of that." She buried her face into her hands. "Oh God. Maybe I am. Maybe I am."

She looked up at me and let go of the stone. It dropped back into her blouse, above her breasts.

"If I am addicted to this evil man, am I as bad as he is? As evil as he is?"

"Do you deal in drugs?" I asked.

"No. I never am involved in his business activities and I never take drugs."

"Do you have people beaten up?

"No."

I fixed my stare on her and finally I asked, "Are you evil, Jade?"

"No, I suppose not, I just don't know how to leave him, other than through death."

"Well, you have just told me that you are not evil, Jade. Maybe you should remember that? Yes?"

"Yes, Robert, thank you, I will. I knew that you would find it impossible to find me a way out; there is no solution, is there?" She was almost imploring me, showing how desperate she was to find a way out.

"We are not here to find solutions, Jade. We are here to offer you emotional support and to allow you to express your feelings in a safe place."

"Yes, I understand," she said with a sad sigh.

"Do you still feel like taking your own life, Jade?"

"No, not now. That feeling comes and goes like the stars in the sky. Other feelings stay with me all the time."

"Do you want to tell me about these other feelings?"

"No, not now. I have a lot to think about." She looked up at the clock on the wall. It was close to 2pm. "I have to go, he will be wondering where I am, I don't want him becoming nasty with me, not today."

She undid the buttons on the cuffs of her blouse and pulled up her sleeves to reveal her thin arms, which were covered in bruises.

"He did this yesterday when he was in a good mood with me. I have to go but I would like to come back to see you again. You have been very good man to talk to, Robert. You have saved me. You are a hero."

I averted my eyes from the bruises and said, "Thanks for saying that, Jade. We are always here on the telephone or you can call in here during the hours of daylight. There will always be someone here."

"Ah, Robert, I don't want someone else, I need to talk to you. When will you be here again?"

"Well, I probably won't be, but you would be able to talk to another volunteer though."

"I want to talk to you, Robert. I need you to talk to you, do you understand, I don't want anyone else. You seem to understand me and no one ever before has spoken to me as you have today, you have been wonderful, so I need you. How about we meet up some time, I can give you a phone number for me that he doesn't know about."

"Jade." I said very firmly. "As a Listening Volunteer I cannot make appointments to see anyone. I also cannot see any caller outside of this branch, it is simply not allowed. It's not just you, Jade, I am not allowed to meet with anyone who calls here, whether by phone or a face-to-face meeting, the way you have called here today. It is not possible and strictly not allowed. I do hope that you understand this."

"Yes, I suppose I will have to understand that, Robert," she said resignedly. "I suppose I do understand it. But I do not have to accept it. Do I? After all, who would know if we were to meet up."

With that, she stood up and walked towards the door.

"Thanks, Robert, you have helped me. I will see you again."

"Good, I am glad that I have been able to help you. If you need us, we are here for you."

I let her out into the street, opened the big blue door for any other callers and then went back up to the Telephone Room. As I was climbing back up the stairs, some of Jade's final words made me shudder. "I do not have to accept it, after all, who would know if we were to meet up", and "I will see you again". No caller had said anything like that to me before, with such determination. I shrugged and thought, *Spur of the moment thoughts. She was emotional.*

Back upstairs, Carl was still sat in the armchair, half asleep.

"Jesus, mate, you look terrible. How are you feeling?" I asked.

"Yes, Robert, not good, I'm fed up that I got drunk and said something to my other half that I shouldn't have said. Bloody drink, I hate it. I just want to go home now, that's all."

"Well, another twenty minutes, mate, and you can do exactly that. Our relief will be here soon. I need to log my face-to-face caller. You're obviously worried over the things that you said last night. I have never seen you look so miserable. All I can say is if you want to talk, well here I am."

"Thanks, Robert. That means a lot. I will go back now and see if I can sort it out, just me and her."

Wow, I thought. Even people like us have problems. I didn't realise it then but my problems were about to start.

By the time I had logged the face-to-face, the relief had arrived, and I handed over my workstation to my fellow volunteer, a very young man, one of the newer Listeners of which there were always plenty. Recruitment continued non-stop.

Carl was beckoning me with his head around the door and a phone in his hand and, as he passed it to me, he said, "It's Bryn. I'm off. Cheers, mate, and thanks."

I gave Carl a wave and answered the call.

"Hi, Bryn," I said.

"How did you get on with your face-to-face, Butt?" the deep Welsh voice asked.

"Okay. It was a young girl stuck in a relationship with someone who is not very nice to be with and she feels trapped. She felt better after letting her feelings out and seemed fine when she left."

I absolutely hated these debriefings. I was determined not to talk about the violence that Jade had experienced nor to tell Bryn that she had asked to meet me outside of the office. I knew that I should have done so but, like Carl, I just wanted to get out of here and over to The Duck to meet the lovely Nicola.

I changed the subject and told Bryn of the veteran from the Falklands War, and what he had told me about the one-armed Argentine and how he had shot the poor lad.

"Quite right, as well," commented Bryn. "Kill the lot of them, I say. They killed a lot of Welsh Guards, you know." Bryn was very non-Listener-like sometimes and was always looking to make reference to his beloved Wales. I did say that I thought the veteran was suffering from PTSD.

Bryn started pontificating about Margaret Thatcher and the Tories, which led me nicely onto the young woman, Jane, who had been forced to become an escort and had prostituted herself so she could feed her kids because of a government cock-up.

I knew that Bryn came from coal-mining stock in South Wales and he was about as left-wing as Joe Stalin, so it got me off the hook as he pontificated about the 'bloody Tories'. Bryn shouldn't have done that and I felt guilty about winding him up. I had waved the red flag at Bryn's bull and it had succeeded in enraging the lefty Welshman.

Bryn was not a good leader as he was too opinionated and, when he started going off on one, he forgot all about the main object of his job, which was to ensure the well-being of the volunteers on his shift. But there was good and bad everywhere.

Chapter Ten

I left the branch and breathed my usual deep breath, the mandatory sigh of relief, on the pavement outside. What a strange morning and now I had to meet up with Nicola, which I would never have dreamt of. What on earth could she want of me? I knew that I was very fond of her, probably too fond. I also knew we got on very well indeed – probably too well. Yes, I found her very attractive and desirable, but she was, as far as I knew, a happily married woman – and that was enough for me.

I walked across the street to The Duck pub and there she was, standing outside, waiting for me. She was wearing a short, light blue cotton dress, the hem of which ended about three inches above her knees; that could be classed as modest for today but I couldn't help thinking that Nicola looked incredibly sexy.

Her beauty was enhanced in the bright sunlight of this wonderful summer's day. All she needed was a flower in her hair and she would make the perfect hippy girl.

"If you're going to San Francisco, be sure to wear some flowers in your hair."

She fitted that song beautifully well. I couldn't help looking at her long, tanned legs, from the short dress to the rope sandals that encased her feet and ankles. Her long, chestnut-brown hair gleamed in the sunlight. I walked across the road towards her.

"Hi, Nic," I said with my usual smile. "I never expected to see you today."

"No," she said. "Nor me you. How are you, Robert?"

I reached her and I was not sure whether to shake her hand or give her a peck on the cheek. So I opted for neither.

"I'm great," she said. "Shall we go inside?"

The Duck was a very large pub owned by one of the bigger pub chains. This Sunday lunchtime it was packed with punters, some finishing their lunch, some starting their lunch. It was a typical modern gastro pub, cavernous in size; this one was originally the old cinema. It had a very long bar with ten staff working behind it, all going flat out to serve the punters who all appeared to be very thirsty on a baking hot day like today. We found a table and I went to the bar and got the drinks: a pint of lager for me and a large glass of pinot grigio for Nicola.

"How was your shift?" she asked.

"It was okay, Nic. A gangster's moll came in on a face to face; she was living in a world of shit because she knew she should leave him but he is controlling her and will not allow her to leave and, anyway, she finally admitted at the end that not only was he addicted to her but she was also addicted to him. I asked her if she was and she surprisingly more or less admitted that she was."

"Not a lot of hope there then," said Nicola.

"No, not a lot. She wanted to meet me for a drink though."

"Bloody hell, Robert, that's dangerous. Did you tell the shift leader? Who was it leading you, Bryn wasn't it?"

"Yes, it was Bryn, and no, I didn't tell him, didn't see the point. You know I hate debriefing. I won't be meeting her, Nicola, please believe me. I ain't that stupid."

"Hope not, Robert," she said, taking a sip of her wine.

"Oh shit, Nic, please believe me."

She smiled at me demurely and then giggled. "For Christ's sake, Robert, of course I believe you."

"Then I took a call from a young mum who has had to prostitute herself because the new Universal Credit meant that her existing benefits were cocked-up."

"Oh no." Nicola had seen it all before but she really was a feminist at heart. Who would not have felt sympathy though for that young mum, Jane, living in a very rich country run by Tories and driven into prostitution by the governing party's incompetence or ignorance, or both?

I continued with my account of the shift.

"Then Carl cracked up on me. Couldn't work the last two hours, he was just sitting there like a zombie."

"What was wrong with Carl? He isn't normally like that."

"Had a heavy night on the booze and had some sort of woman trouble. I don't really know too much about it, apart from the fact that he was well messed up."

"Oh, I thought he was living with someone."

"Well, he should know better. Best off on your own, no hassle. Well, then, only … maybe sometimes you feel a bit, you know … a bit …"

"A bit what, Robert?" Her big brown eyes were fixed on me in a way that made me feel uncomfortable.

I looked down at the table and then up at her and I noticed she was not wearing any make-up. She didn't need any, I thought, and then I replied, "A bit lonely sometimes. Maybe." I finally admitted this with some reluctance.

"You can actually be in a relationship and sometimes feel lonely, Robert."

She had placed her arms on the table, they were tanned to match her legs, and I wondered if she was tanned all over. I knew that I shouldn't think like this but being near Nicola made me feel that way, especially now that we were out of the branch, with all its restrictions. It was more relaxed here and she was so bloody desirable. Nicola would, in all likelihood, make a bloody monk feel and think like that.

"Where is your husband today, Nic?"

"At his mother's. So, he says. I didn't want to go and sit with his dad, who is a bank manager like my husband. David, my husband, always wanted to follow in his dad's footsteps. David's mum, with her dutiful wifey outlook on life, doesn't like me much, well, not at all really. We once had a row and I called her a boring, stuck-up old hag. We didn't speak for a year and barely do now. I'm not good enough for her son in her eyes. Do you want another drink, Robert?" she asked, and without waiting for an answer she headed off to the bar.

I was surprised to hear Nicola talk of her private life in this way and I was beginning to think that maybe she wasn't as happily married as I had first thought. I watched her walk up to the bar. God, she looked gorgeous. Tall and tanned, slim and lovely, just like the Girl from Ipanema.

Why did she want me to meet her? I would find out soon enough. She would inevitably tell me in her own time.

She came back with the drinks and her long brown hair swept down across her face as she sat down, and she pushed it back with her hands.

"There we go. I suppose you were surprised to receive a text from me."

"I was, Nic, yes, to be honest. Is everything okay?"

"Good, yes. I was just wondering how you have been since the call you took on Thursday morning, the suicide in progress. It seemed to affect you and I was concerned at the time. Matter of fact, Robert, I have been worried ever since. It seemed to hit you for six. Have you been all right since then? You know, I have to say, that all I wanted to do before I left you was give you a big hug. You looked so down, so low after the call. I really felt for you."

"Well, that's so strange, Nicola, because all I wanted to do was the same to you. I really needed a hug then. Only from you though." I was embarrassed again now.

"I know, Robert, I understand. Maybe we have a bond. Maybe we should be careful."

"Oh." I was truly surprised at this. If anyone was listening to our conversation, they may say I sounded disappointed. "Careful of what, Nicola?"

"Well, you know what it's like, it's always a pleasure to work with you. No, it's a joy to work a shift with you. We seem to have an understanding, we seem to just, well you know … click. I work with other guys and I never feel as close to them as I do to you."

"I understand exactly what you are saying, Nicola. But why should we be careful?"

"Because we might be wandering blindly towards something that would not be good for me or you. You know what it's like. Emotions in that place." She pointed across the road to the branch. "Emotions run high. Suppose your call from the suicidal lady had happened earlier in the shift and it had ended with ninety minutes to go before the relief got there and we had hugged. How would you have felt then, Robert, being completely alone with me?"

"I would have found it extremely difficult to let you go, Nicola, if you want to know the truth. I would have hung on for dear life and bled you dry of your emotions. Sorry, but that is how it would have been, seeing that you asked."

She looked at me with her unique stare, an honest stare.

"Exactly, and because of how I felt for you at that moment, maybe I could not have let you go. I'm an old married woman, Robert." She laughed and I thought I saw a tear in her eye and she wiped her hand across her face. "All be it a very unhappily married old woman."

"I didn't realise. Is that why you are here alone and he, your husband, is at his mother's?"

She answered directly, staring strongly at me, "Yes."

I was struggling to find the courage but, finally, I asked her if she had children. It was the first time that I had asked her a personal question.

"God, no," she said. "I can't have children."

I was shocked at this, I didn't realise; we had spent hours together working our shifts and I didn't really know a lot about her. We Listeners very rarely asked personal questions of one another. I knew she was married, knew that her husband was a banker but that was it.

"I had to ask, Nic, sorry to hear your answer. Is your husband okay with the situation?"

"With what situation, Robert?"

"Oh God, sorry, I shouldn't have asked."

"No, we will be divorced soon. He will come back later and tell me that he is moving to his mother's while we sell our house and we can both downsize, you know, buy a smaller house each and go our separate ways and that will be that after eleven years of marriage. He wants a child and I can't give him that, so I am put out to pasture like the old barren cow that I am and he can find someone else to give him his child, to carry his child and his mother's precious grandchild. Do I sound bitter? Oh, bloody hell, Robert, I hope I don't sound bitter, not now. A bitter and twisted, barren old cow. I am forty you know?"

It was her turn to look down now. I desperately wanted to hug her again then.

"I am so sorry, Nic," I said. "I had no idea that this was happening to you. Are you okay? What a stupid question." I held my hands up resignedly. "I just had to ask, that's all."

"Yes, Robert, I'm okay, it's just a shame, in many ways, but I haven't loved him since I became a Listener. The organisation changes everyone to a degree, doesn't it? We hear of so much tragedy. Then, sometimes the situations that we hear of makes us think of our own lives and, if something is not right, then the things that we have heard seem to highlight our own unhappiness, our own difficulties."

We both sat in silence for a short while until she broke the ice.

"Tell me more about your suicidal lady please, Robert. If you want to. If you can cope with it. I didn't want to push you when we had our coffee the other morning, but I was hoping maybe you could say something now. She sounds remarkable and I don't even know anything about the call."

"Oh, yes. The lady did make me think quite a bit about my own life. But I have been alright since Thursday, it just got a bit emotional, that's all."

"Yes, I understand. I love listening to you speak to the callers. You really do connect with them in a big way, Robert. You are becoming quite accomplished at that fine art. I love it and when I listen to you speak, I am envious. I wish I could get into the callers as you do."

"Well, thanks for that, all I do is try my best, Nic. I couldn't stop the lady from dying, she was too far gone when she phoned and, more importantly, it was her will to die, her wish. She was quite a lady though, name of … well let's not go there, her name doesn't matter. What mattered to me was that she reminded me of me. She said that she 'Ran through life grabbing big chunks of it and ate it all up'. That is what I was like once. Totally selfish." My hands were folded on top of the table and Nicola reached out and placed her hand over mine and squeezed it.

"You're not selfish," she said.

Her hand stayed where it was for a few seconds and all I could feel was a tingling running down the back of my neck. I looked up at her face, with those big brown eyes, and smiled. We said nothing, just looked at one another. Finally, I had to avert my gaze because I really wanted Nicola now. There was an electric storm brewing and she was also playing her part in making the thunder and lightning commence. Embarrassed, I looked away and stared towards some people standing close by and I saw a familiar face amongst the throng of people, staring at me and at Nicola. It was the Vietnamese girl Jade, my face-to-face caller.

She was standing next to a tall man with dyed blonde hair. She stood staring at us for what felt like a long time but was probably no more than two seconds. Then the man with the dyed hair put his hand on her shoulder and guided her towards the door. They disappeared into the crowd. Nicola had removed her hand and was staring at me.

"Let's have another," I suggested. She nodded; she had not noticed that my attention had been diverted elsewhere.

"Do you know how old I am?" she asked, when I returned with the drinks.

"Yes, of course I do. Forty."

She looked surprised.

"How did you know that?"

"You just told me," I laughed. "Earlier, when you called yourself a barren old cow."

"Oh, did I? I didn't realise. Yes, I'm getting old."

"Christ, Nic, you don't look old, you look like a young girl in her early twenties, a proper hippy."

"Thank you, Robert. I always loved you," she said, tongue in cheek. "It's my dark skin, it makes me look younger. You're fifty-five," she said.

"How did you know that? Listen, I don't do numbers, they mean nothing. I may be officially fifty-five, but I feel loads younger. I'm fit and above all else happy, that makes me feel younger than I am. Being sat here with you today with your beauty makes me feel even younger."

"Wow!" she said. "Thanks for that, you old charmer. Anyway, to answer your question, you told me. How did you think I knew? Witchcraft?" she laughed.

"Maybe," I joked.

"Were you ever married, Robert?"

"No, never. I came close to it, to the mother of my daughter, in another life, it seems like now. I was eighteen at the time."

"So young," she said with that big warm grin. "Young love is wonderful."

"Maybe it is, Nic, but it is also sometimes foolish."

We started to become slightly tipsy as we chatted and laughed until she looked at her watch and said she would have to go, as her husband would be home soon. It was gone five and we had been talking for three hours. Time had passed really quickly. I looked at her in a concerned sort of way. "Will you be all right at home, Nicola?"

"Yes, I will be fine. We need to get this sorted, my husband and I. No one else can help us. We need to grow up and stop playing the game of being happily married when we're not and we need … both of us need to get on with the rest of our lives."

"Will you be okay living alone, Nicola? It's a bit different being alone after a long marriage."

She looked at me again and sighed. "I can only say to you, Robert, in all honesty, that I have been living with a man for eleven years, have been married to that man for eleven years and there have been times in that eleven years that I have felt alone. Completely alone. So, I now return to our loveless, cold four-bedroom house, to live alone. I have been married, but alone, for a very long time, Robert, and we have not shared a bed for more than a year now. And, yes, I am lonely and alone, so the future can only get better."

"I can beat that; I haven't slept with a woman for nearly two-and-a-half years. What about that, Nic?"

"I would never have believed that, Robert. You seem like Jack the Lad in many ways."

"I was, but that ended a long time ago. The organisation changed me like the organisation changed you."

She smiled at me again. "I have to go, Robert. I would love to stay here with you, but I must go now to confront reality."

I felt so sorry for the situation that Nicola was now in. I looked at her, reached for her hand and said, with all the feelings of love and friendship that I could muster, "I am here for you, Nicola. Here if you need me."

It was my turn to squeeze her hand now. She smiled back at me and I noticed the tears were still in her big brown eyes. She said, "I know, Robert. I know, and thank you."

She had to catch the Tube and I escorted her to the station, fighting off the desire to hold her hand. We stood outside the main entrance and she said, "I really enjoyed that, Robert. It was so good to talk and I wish I didn't have to go but, well, you know how it is."

She turned to look at me and old Jack the Lad was melted. I felt that I was beginning to love her – or was it desire? Which was it? Probably a mixture of both, if the truth were told.

She leant forward and kissed me gently on the lips. I could feel the softness of her lips on mine and I nearly passed out; I felt heady. That kiss blew me away. I was not expecting it, and it was beautiful. I touched her arm and she shuddered and she put her arms around my neck and pulled my head closer to her. I could smell her and, as I kissed her, I could taste her. My hands moved to her back and I could feel her body under her thin cotton dress, my fingers felt the muscles in her back. I squeezed her closer to me. This was becoming intimate, I thought, as my heartbeat doubled. I had always loved working with this woman, I had always felt close to her in our shared commitment to the organisation, and now I was as close to her as I had ever been. I was touching her body, albeit through her clothing. I wished that the thin layer of clothing was not there. She pulled herself away.

"I have to go, Robert. We're on the 2am shift on Tuesday morning. I will see you then."

She slowly let go of my hand, turned and ran away towards the station entrance. As I watched her go, I noticed someone glaring at me. It was Jade. She stood there, not more than four metres away, just staring at me, with her cold eyes boring into me. Then she gave me an evil smile. I shivered. She turned and disappeared into the Tube station.

I was stunned and just stood there staring after this strange foreign beauty who had walked into my life. I felt a dark cloud looming over me.

"Oh, bloody hell!" I said in despair. "What is happening to me now?"

Part Four

The Storm Breaks

Chapter Eleven

It was 1.45am on the Tuesday morning, two days after we had met in The Duck. Nicola and I were chatting in the phone room to the two Listeners who had just worked the 10pm to 2am shift, who we were relieving. Freddie and Trudy were two of the younger volunteers, both in their early twenties. They looked so young, I thought, but the input which these younger-generation Listeners made to the cause was very important because their contribution was a vital part in ensuring the branch could stay open for twenty-four hours a day, which was our ultimate aim. Every day! Judging by their numbers, 2346 and 2348, they had joined at the same time and completed their training together. It was common for the trainees to bond and I envied them this as there was no one left of my intake; they had all fallen by the wayside and left.

Freddie was worried about the number of SNAP calls he had experienced during the shift and was wondering whether or not it was anything to do with his voice. It was rather high-pitched but I knew that was nothing to do with it. Luck was what it was all about. If someone phones who is desperate to speak to a Listener, then they will speak. Callers hang up for a variety of reasons.

Nicola was trying to console him on this and was saying that he shouldn't worry about such things; SNAP calls were commonplace in the overall experience; we all had them and we could all deal with it in our own way.

Trudy told us the air conditioning wasn't working in the phone room and it was bloody hot. They were interrupted by the kitchen phone ringing and Freddie and Trudy went to answer it, as they knew it was their leader. Nicola smiled at me and asked if I wanted a coffee. I declined and she went to make one for herself. I went to Listening Station B, near the window, and logged myself in. I was reading the notes left on the computer whiteboard when Nicola came back in. I looked up at her. She was wearing baggy cotton trousers and a white long-sleeved collarless shirt that was probably two sizes too big for her. This was the first time we had been alone together since our parting outside the Tube station, and the memory of that kiss was still very much with me. It seemed as though something unfinished was simmering between us. I was detecting a change in the way that she looked at me, it seemed different, but I was absolutely sure I was looking at her in the same way. We both seemed short of breath and I knew it had nothing to do with the lack of air conditioning. There was a tension building between us and it was not an uncomfortable tension.

She went to her normal work station and was logging herself in when she looked around at me and said, "They've gone. Wished you a happy shift, bless them. How are you, Robert?"

"Fine," I said. "More importantly, how have you been? How did you get on when you got home from the pub on Sunday?"

"Do you mean with my husband? Well, that was complicated at first. But then in a very civilised way we agreed to divide our assets evenly and break up in a civilised way. I will see a lawyer in the week and so will he. We've put the house on the market and he left that night to stay with his mum. While I was at work yesterday all of his possessions, including some of the furniture, were removed from the house. The house isn't completely empty but it's a strange experience."

"I can relate to that," I said. "When I got back from the Falklands I went home to a completely empty house. It hit me for six, I can tell you, so I really do sympathise, Nic."

"I didn't know you were in the Falklands, Robert."

"I didn't know that you went to work, Nicola."

"I'm a school teacher. I told you before, Robert, didn't I?"

"Well, I'll be damned. A school teacher. No, I don't think you told me that. We mentioned work when we had coffee down by the river but you didn't actually tell me what you did."

I got up and went to sit in the armchair that was behind me and next to Nicola's desk. It's where I always sat if I wanted to speak to my shift buddies.

"That's better, I can see you now," I said as I sat down.

"There is probably a lot that we don't know of one another," she said.

"Nicola, you are going through a lot at the moment, what with your divorce and everything, and I am trying not to sound like a counsellor, but are you alright?"

"Well, mate, not really," she said. "It is sad, even though I don't love him, it … well, it was a long while to be with someone …"

She looked down at the floor. I thought she was going to burst into tears and I didn't know what to do. Here we were, alone in this room in the early hours of the morning, and I was feeling so sad for this woman, my friend. I felt an empathy for this beautiful woman that I had never felt for any other person before.

Nicola continued her sad tale. "But that isn't all of it. During our discussions on Sunday, which we had to conduct sat around our dining room table, which will sit twelve people but we haven't used for two years or more, it became the boardroom table. He is, as you know, a bank manager, so business has to be conducted in a proper and professional manner, so he says, and as usual he got his way. He was sat at one end and me at the other, like we were negotiating a massive business loan."

What a prick, I thought.

"How did it go?" I asked her.

"Yes, it went well, as I said before. The house and a couple of insurance policies were all sorted, as well all the financial matters, which were arranged amicably without any major arguments. All went well until we came to the end of the fucking board meeting." I had never heard her swear like that before.

"What happened then?"

"Well, he announced that he had not loved me for a long time, which frankly, Robert, I knew anyway, and he said that he has felt this way for five years or more, about the time I was trying fertility treatment." She stopped and blew her nose.

I looked at her and said quietly, "Are you sure it's you, Nic? Do you actually know that it is you're problem that you can't have children? It takes two to tango, mate."

"Oh, yes, it's definitely me. We both had tests and he was fine. You should have seen him strutting around like bloody Rambo when his results came through. Telling me that it was my mother's fault for not feeding me properly when I was a small girl." She seemed ashamed. "I guessed then that he hated me for not being able to have children and I guessed then that he was seeing other women, which is what he confirmed on Sunday night."

She looked so low. I didn't know whether to give her a hug, but I thought it would be better to let her continue.

She sighed and said, "So, he's been seeing someone else for six months now. She's twenty-eight and absolutely able to have children. New blood, new young blood, while me the barren old cow is shoved out to pasture. I know, Robert, that I'm sounding bitter again and I apologise."

"I'm so sorry, Nicola, to see you like this and I don't know what else I can say, other than I'm sure that everything will work out for you. Please realise that you are a very beautiful girl, inside and out, and we all love you."

She was wiping her eyes as the tears came. I was unsure of what to do. Then my hands reached out for her. I was sitting too far away to touch her, but I just held my hands out, palms open, just beckoning to her. She got up from her seat, in her bare feet and baggy shirt and trousers, and walked towards me. She was breathing faster, and so was I as she took my hands in her own and sat in the chair with me. She was straddling me, her knees either side of my thighs on the seat and I put my arms around her. She moved towards me and we hugged each other very tightly, her face next to my left cheek. I could feel the wetness of the tears on her face. I held her tight and she was holding me as though she would never let go. I could feel her body moving with every breath she took and we stayed this way for a long time. I could smell her skin, the fragrance of scented soap, and her shampooed hair.

She turned her head towards me and I looked into her eyes, which were free of tears now; she was moving her head towards mine and she kissed me, just like she'd done outside the Tube station, softly, gently. I could taste her again and I felt her breathing getting faster, in sync with my own, as our kisses became more passionate. She was sucking at my lips and I responded, tugging at her lips with my own. She held me at the back of my neck with her right hand and I was running my hands up and down her beautiful back, feeling those wonderful muscles through the thin shirt she was wearing. My tongue entered her mouth and she welcomed me.

Her hand was on my chest now and I moved my hands slowly down the length of her back to take hold of her buttocks, and I drew her to me. Then I stopped and held her by her arms. She looked at me in bewilderment.

"Nicola," I said, "you are beautiful but you are also very vulnerable right now. Are you sure this is what you want?"

She let out a deep breath and I could feel it on my face as she still straddled me.

"Robert, this is nothing to do with what is going on between me and my stupid husband, this is about you and me, and this was always going to happen."

I sat back and wanted to say more. She was trying to say something but stopped mid-sentence as she bent down towards me and kissed my lips, silencing me. I reached out for her. I could feel her and I realised that I could touch this woman on any part of her body, even her most intimate places, and I would be welcomed.

My hands were moving all over her body and I felt as though I wanted to belong to her, to couple with her, be part of her. She responded to my every touch by shuddering or emitting small groans of pleasure. I knew then that this was a very sensitive and sensual woman. I felt her fingers at the back of my neck and I could taste her and smell her as my mouth opened to her and, again, I felt an overwhelming desire. I wanted to eat her, devour her as we kissed in the most passionate of ways. I felt her touching me underneath my shirt and my hands moved beneath hers and, for the first time, I felt the silkiness and the softness of her skin; her naked body beneath my hands, her hands moving over me now as I lifted up her baggy shirt, pulling it over her head as she did the same to me.

She was wearing no bra and my head bent down towards her perfectly rounded breasts. I licked and bit at her nipples and again she responded to the sensuality of my tongue, squirming and thrusting her breasts out to me. Her hands reached for my trousers and fumbled with the belt on my jeans, while I was gorging myself on her body. She was moaning quietly, a moan of pure pleasure and desire. I felt the hardness pressing against my jeans and I could feel her hand now on my penis as she rubbed and caressed it, loving the organ that we both knew would be inside her very soon.

I knew then that we had passed the point of no return. We were set on our course of a passionate journey that we knew would end with an explosive climax. My lips were back on hers and our tongues moved around each other's open mouths as her hard nipples ground into my bare chest. My hands were on her buttocks again, feeling them through the thin cotton trousers, feeling the outline of her panties, which aroused me to a greater level.

My fingers caressed her vagina through the thin material and we started to lose control. Suddenly she was off the chair and standing in front of me, with tiny rivulets of sweat running down between her breasts. She was glistening, coated in the moisture generated by the room temperature and the fire of our passion.

I watched as she pulled down her trousers and her panties. Her mouth was open as though she was struggling to breathe in her state of fervour. She tugged at my trainers, pulling them off, and she reached for my trousers, which were already open at the fly. She hauled them off as fast as she could, almost in a frenzy, and cast them aside. I sat there, my erection waving at her, and she stood naked in front of me; that dark naturally tanned body with her nipples erect and the neat dark patch of shaved hair between her legs.

She stood still for a brief moment. Her breathing was fast and almost laboured, as was mine. Mentally we resembled two prize fighters in the ring, combatants who focused their whole world on each other before making their next move; at that moment in time, this analogy was Nicola and I. But we were not combatants, we were lovers about to engage in a frenzied bout of sensuality, and there would be an end result to this.

We fixated our stares and our thoughts, concentrating totally on each other before making our next move. I broke this brief impasse. She was standing in front of me, this dark-skinned gorgeous beauty, glistening in sweat and, as I reached out and pulled her towards me, my hand moved between her legs to her most private warm place. She started to writhe on my hand, making small groans. I said to her, in an almost breathless voice, "I want to kiss you here."

I licked my lips and she moved toward me as I lay back in the armchair. Both her feet were either side of me on the chair seat and her hands were gripping the back of the chair either side of my head as she moved the most intimate part of her body towards my waiting tongue. I felt the chair move backwards and we almost toppled over. She cried out as my tongue found her most sensitive place and she squirmed upon me and I sucked at her. I tasted her juices and thrust my face at her until she collapsed breathless onto my lap and opened herself to me. I could feel myself sliding into her and we were rocking in our ecstasy. We were as one, joined together in a world of sexual intensity that both of us had not experienced for a very long time.

The love famine which we had both endured for years seemed to drive us to further heights of ecstasy, and I felt as though I would burst. Nicola drove us both beyond control as she held onto my arms, leaning back and moving rhythmically, with me inside her. She was impaled upon me and we were joined together. Her body gleamed and glistened in the subdued lighting and her long hair was hanging back behind her, almost touching the floor as she abandoned herself to me in an overwhelming passion, which by now had completely taken control of her mind and body. I held on to her as she leant backwards knowing that, if I let her slip, she would topple onto the floor, where no doubt this whirlwind of almost violent activity would continue. I could feel these seismic events coming to a climax. I looked past her to the wall opposite and my eyes fixed on the portrait of the Listeners' Organisation's founder, the Reverend Moore, who seemed to be staring down in disbelief and shock at the sight of two of his faithful disciples locked in a mind-blowing frenzy of sexual fever. Here, within his temple.

Nicola leant forward and all thoughts and images of the good reverend disappeared from my mind as our lips met and our tongues explored each other's mouths as we both emitted groans and small cries of love. Our perspiration mixed and blended together as she grasped at me, and I was holding her as though I could never let her go. I held her tighter, crushing her to me as I felt her tighten around my cock, and she exploded onto me with short sharp screams of passion and pleasure as I pumped all my juices into her, I marvelled at what had taken place between us. Passionate and perfect sexual union.

We lay still, holding each other, our heavy breathing easing as we slowly recovered our calmness and the passion subsided into total exhaustion. We could feel the wetness of our sweat sticking us together like a bonding adhesive and I could feel all of the love juices trickling from within her onto my body. She was sobbing very gently and I held her until we both very slowly subsided into peacefulness after the violent frenzy which we had both experienced. Then we were lost in a beautiful sleep together.

I was not sure how long we slept. When I came to my senses I forgot where I was and then Nicola stirred and I realised I was in an armchair in the Telephone Room of the Welford Branch of the Listeners' Organisation with a beautiful naked woman lying on top of me. I have in my time woken up in some very strange and wonderful places, with all manner of female partners, but I could not remember any other similar scenario being as wonderful as that one. I turned my head to her and kissed her hair and I thought that I would like to repeat our experience here and now. I touched her body, still slippery with sweat, and then I glanced at the clock above me and saw it was 3.22am.

Bloody hell! Over an hour into our shift and we had taken no calls at all; however, we had been somewhat busy. Nicola stirred on top of me and seemed to be awake. I looked at her face with her dark hair matted to it. She smiled at me and said in her husky voice, "Oh Robert, what have we done?"

These were her only words as she pushed herself up out of the chair, her dark body still glistening in sweat as she gathered up her discarded clothing and strolled out to the kitchen. I could hear a tap running in the kitchen and the door slam as she went out to the toilet. I smiled at the thought of her wandering around the branch naked.

I gathered up my own clothes and put them back on. The leather chair was wet with sweat but it could easily be wiped off.

Nicola came back into the room fully clothed and looked at me nervously, almost sheepishly, then she walked over to me, kissed my cheek and said, "Thank you, Robert, that was beautiful. I never thought I would experience that feeling again."

She held out her hands in a gesture of resignation. "I couldn't have dreamt it."

She smiled her big gorgeous smile, her white teeth gleaming like polished pearls.

I looked at her and said, "What didn't you dream, Nic?"

"Well, I didn't dream or expect that. What I can only call total abandonment to pure unadulterated sex, that's what I am trying to say. Don't forget I am supposed to be the barren old cow put out to grass. The middle-aged frumpy school teacher, only good for being a teacher."

I looked up at her and smiled. I really wanted to hold her again.

"Well, Nicola, you are certainly no barren, frumpy school teacher. You are bloody well gorgeous and alive and vibrant and a most ardent, passionate lover; you made me feel so good that I should be thanking you. I didn't even think that I would ever get it up again, let alone experience something like that, and you made it happen. You are wonderful."

I thought she would burst into tears. She came to me and kissed me on the lips and whispered, "Thank you, Robert, thanks for saying that. You brought something back to life in me, something that I thought was dead and buried."

I said, "I think that has been on the cards for a while now. You knew there was a mutual attraction between us, the way we worked together, the way we were together, there's no denying it, Nic. Well, now my gorgeous angel, I think we just proved it."

"I know," she said. "I've been feeling that way for a while now; you know, really close to you."

She raised her hand to her mouth and almost bent double in laughter as she said, "Oh, bloody hell, Robert, and for that to happen in here of all places. Christ, it's a good job there are no cameras in here – that would have been hot stuff."

"Yes, and with the reverend looking on as well," I said, pointing up at the portrait of the organisation's founder.

"Oh my God, yes, I never thought about him. We need to show respect in future and have our nooky elsewhere, not in here, Robert, it's wrong. Lovely, but wrong."

I smiled back at her, encouraged that she had acknowledged there would be another time. I shrugged.

"Do you really think that was the first time two people have made love in this room, Nicola? This place has been used by our organisation since 1966, so do you really think we are the first?"

"I … I never thought about it."

"Well, there have been men and women working in here together for the last fifty-one years in the most tense and emotional circumstances. Do you not think that at some stage, during the last half-century, two volunteers who were attracted to each other haven't let their emotions run out of control before today?"

I looked at her and then I answered my own question. "Of course, they have. No one talks about it, we are confidential. We are Listeners."

We both laughed at this.

"It's now three thirty and we haven't taken any calls. How do we explain that one away, Nic?"

"I doubt if anyone will notice but we could cover ourselves by saying that I was taken ill with stomach cramps shortly after we started and you went to the Tesco all-night store to get me paracetamol. You were worried about me and cared for me, which you did." Again, she was grinning at me. "I don't think we should do a shift at night again, Robert, I really don't."

"Why on earth not?"

"Because that may happen again and, as I said earlier, it's not right. Not in here, Robert. Come on, you know it. We should be here for the callers and nothing else."

"Well, I would like to make love to you again any place we can." I pointed up to the portrait of the Reverend Moore. "As we said earlier, I don't think he would approve though, so I do understand."

I hoped I didn't sound too sulky. All I knew was that I wanted Nicola again and again; if I had awoken some hidden passion in her then she had definitely achieved the same in me. I wanted her all to myself. *Is the selfishness of Robert reappearing*? I wondered.

She took hold of my hands, I embraced her and smelt the rawness of her and I felt myself becoming aroused again. She detected this and said, "Down boy. Come on, let's listen to the callers."

"Nicola, we probably need to talk to one another at some stage. Why don't you come back to my place after this shift?"

"I would love to," she said, "but I can't. The estate agent is bringing people around to look at the house at ten o'clock and I have to be there. Then, this afternoon, I have to go to see my mum in Manchester. I need to explain what happened between David and me. She doesn't know we've split yet and she will be devastated. She really loved David. As it's nearing the end of term, I thought it would be a good time to spend some quality time with her, so I have taken some leave. The headmaster knows about the break-up of my marriage and has been brilliant about it. He told me to take the rest of the term off and to come back in September."

"When are you back?" I asked sadly.

"In a week. Next Thursday. Unless I stay on."

"Oh, okay. I know you need to get things sorted out and I know telling your mum is important, so I do understand. It's just that … well, I want you to know that what happened between us here tonight is important to me and you are important to me, and I want to see you again. Do you know what I mean?"

"Of course. I understand, Robert. It was more than a quick shag to me as well, obviously. I have never done quick shags anyway, I'm not that type, but the thing that just happened here between us means a lot to me too, as it does you. I promise we can meet as soon as I get back, I will message you, I promise. What I will say to you though is that I don't want to become involved in another relationship right now. I can't anyway because it's so soon after David for me to become embroiled in something else so quickly. I do hope you understand this, Robert. I didn't expect to have sex with another man, not ever again, for me it seemed an impossibility. But sex isn't the be all and end all of any relationship. I think we have all the ingredients, but this is not the time."

"That's fine. I totally agree with you. I don't need a relationship either. I just think the world of you, that's all. Let's see how it goes."

I spoke these words as though I meant them, full of sincerity, but underneath I knew it was cobblers. I wanted a repeat performance of what had just happened here and I no longer wanted to live alone. I wanted to be with her, Nicola … Nicola 1880.

I don't even know her surname, I thought. *How bizarre is that. I probably love her and I don't even know her name, only that she is Nicola 1880.*

"I'm sure everything will work out for you, Nic."

"Thanks, Robert. Now come on, let's take some calls."

She kissed me on the lips and we both got ourselves ready to deal with the great British public. I clicked on 'Start taking calls' and the phone immediately rang.

"Can I help?"

Chapter Twelve

I was back on shift the following Monday, six days after Nicola and I had made love in the phone room. I was working the afternoon shift from 2pm to 6.30pm. As I walked into the room I looked longingly at the armchair where we had done the unthinkable and it made me sad because I missed Nicola. She had texted me on Saturday and told me she was staying with her mum for another 'few' days. It was a pretty short message and I wondered whether she really did have any feelings for me, and I felt more than a little hurt.

I know I'm selfish, but what we had shared that hot night was so good that I just longed for more of her. I was becoming besotted and I knew this was not fair on Nicola because she had a lot on her plate. I was also fifteen years older than her – not that she seemed to mind that last Tuesday. Maybe she was just frustrated and had used me to vent her feelings of frustration. She did put everything into it and I remembered how sexually crazy she had become. I became ashamed of myself for even thinking that.

Another strange thing had occurred yesterday. I had been at the fishing lake all day and when I returned, at around 10pm, I found a card which had been posted through the letterbox of my apartment block. Someone, a neighbour obviously, had placed it into my pigeon hole. It was a thank-you card and I read the words: *I will always be grateful to you Robert. From the lady with the green stone*. A mobile phone number was written below with an instruction for me to phone it straight away. I tore the card into pieces and binned it. The sender could only have been the Vietnamese girl, Jade; the girl with the green stone.

I was flabbergasted and shocked. She must have followed me home at some stage to know where I lived. I had spotted her a couple of times since our face-to-face meeting in the branch over a week ago – while I was in The Duck pub with Nicola and then again at the Tube station, when I had caught her staring at me after I'd first kissed Nicola. I remembered her strange, frightening smile and how she slowly and deliberately turned on her heel and disappeared into the station.

Oh God, I thought. *What is happening?* I was shaking and felt odd. I was becoming stressed. I had never felt like this and I just wanted it to go away.

I was at my usual place by the window and I looked over at my shift buddy. Today, it was a very young girl, called Libby, who was around twenty years old and had just become a probationary Listener. This was her first solo shift without her mentor. We had chatted before the shift started and she told me how nervous she was feeling. All I could say to her was, "Remember your training and stick to it and you'll be fine." She was nervous but enthusiastic. She was a chubby, blonde-haired student at the local college, training to be a nurse. Libby oozed innocence in her flowered dress. She was speaking on the phone to a caller and was totally absorbed.

I turned to my work station and clicked on 'Start taking calls'. I looked up at the clock, 4pm. The phone rang immediately, making me jump. I was edgy, and had been so since finding that card yesterday.

"Can I help?"

A young-sounding female voice said, "Hello."

I had heard only one word but I already knew this person was frightened.

"Can I help you?"

"Yes, I need help."

"Okay, don't worry now, we are here to help, here for you. Can you tell me why you need help?"

"I just do."

"Has something in particular happened to you recently that made you want to phone us today."

"No, not really, it's just that everything is wrong with my life."

"Is there any one thing that is wrong above everything else?"

I could hear a mechanical noise like an approaching jet aircraft, and then a blast of a horn and a whoosh of what I recognised as a train passing by. The rattling of the wheels on the tracks and the vibrating noise as it passed by sounded incredibly loud. I could picture my caller turning away from the invasion of her peace as this mechanical juggernaut thundered past.

"Hello," I said. "Are you still there?"

"Yes, I'm still here." The caller sounded tired.

"Obviously you are near a railway line." Just the thought of saying those words made me shudder.

"Yes, I'm at a railway station."

"Okay, are you intending to travel somewhere?"

"No, not really, I ... well, I just came here. The station is in the countryside, and I saw your number on the entrance gate, so I phoned you. There's no one else here."

Her voice sounded shrill and very young. It was interesting that the caller mentioned the organisation's number being displayed on the entrance to the station. I knew that this number, together with a short message, was displayed at most railway stations and high bridges throughout the UK, in an effort to prevent suicides.

"That's fine. You told me earlier that everything had gone wrong in your life. Would you like to tell me a little bit about what has happened?"

"I'm sick of it, Mister, sick of everything about my life. Sick of where I live, which is a shit-hole, and sick of having no money."

"It sounds as though you are going through a rough time. Are there other things that bother you?"

"Everything went wrong when they put Buddy away."

"Can I ask, please, who is Buddy?"

"He's my boyfriend. He got stitched up with a drug scam. Framed by his own brother he was, and now he's in jail because of them. He didn't do anything and life is shit and I'm fed up with it. Buddy hates it in jail and he's in for two years and he can't handle it. It's horrible in there and he's already been beaten up Mister. They just went in his cell and punched and kicked him, because he didn't have any of that spice stuff that they all take in there."

"Do you mean the drug spice?"

"Yeah, that's it, they get it smuggled inside and Buddy, he told them that he could get it but they would have to pay him some money first and then they fucked up on the delivery. Buddy got the blame and it ain't fair cos they went and beat up on him, Mister, it just ain't fair!"

Organisations like the Samaritans have a presence in UK prisons, where they listen to prisoners' problems and counsel them. They had done a wonderful job until the government, in its wisdom, cut the professional Listening service that was always present in prisons, resulting in an increase in suicides.

I had heard of spice from various news reports. It consists of marijuana leaves sprayed with some sort of chemical, and it was very widely used throughout the country's prison system; it was also known as the Zombie Drug because people who use it turn into zombies. It takes them into a world of hallucinations, panic attacks and violent behaviour. Users will lose days of their lives in a coma, which the prisoners desire to relieve the boredom of their incarceration.

Buddy sounded like a bit of a bad boy; he had only been inside a short time and was already dealing in drugs. I doubted if this girl's initial assertion that Buddy was innocent was true, but it wasn't for me to judge. But it sounded as though Buddy had a great influence on this caller's life. I needed to find out more.

"How did you find out about this?"

"Well, he phoned me, Mister. He has a phone in the jail."

"Okay and how does it affect you when he phones you?"

"Well, I fucking love it, don't I. What a stupid question, he is my man."

"Okay, sorry if you didn't like my question."

"Oh, that's okay, I just feel like shit at the minute, Mister."

"I'm so sorry to hear that, you obviously miss Buddy."

"Course I do, Mister, I can't live without him. We have our names tattooed on our arms, Kim and Buddy, in a great big heart."

"Can I call you Kim?"

"Yeah, if you want."

"Can I ask you, Kim, why are you at the railway station?"

"Oh, Mister, why do think I am at the fucking railway station? I'm waiting for a fucking train!"

"Do you have any intention of harming yourself, Kim?"

"Yes, Mister, I do. Buddy will kill himself in jail and I will die here."

"Do you have a pact?"

"Yep, I'm doing it now in front of a fucking train and, when he is told about me, he will hang himself and …"

There was another explosion of sound as another high-speed train went hurtling through the station. Then I heard the noise of a small baby crying.

"Do you have someone with you, Kim?"

"Yeah, that fucking train woke her up."

"You have your baby with you? Am I right, Kim?"

"Yes, Mister, you're right."

"I have to ask you, Kim, I'm sort of wondering … why have you brought your baby with you to the railway station?"

"To be with me, of course."

"To be with you when you jump? Is that what you mean, Kim?"

"Yeah, she has to be. Don't she. She does, Mister!"

"Do you want your baby to die, Kim?"

"No, of course not, but we have to go together otherwise what will happen to her? My Poppy."

"Can I ask how old you are, Kim?"

"Oh, don't fucking start, Mister. I'm twenty, alright, I just sound young on the phone, everyone says that. Poppy is nine months, aren't you, darling?" She was talking to the baby now.

The fact that Kim had a baby with her changed everything, and the Safeguarding Act for Children would come into play. Under the laws of safeguarding, although not obliged to intervene, we can do so by getting the appropriate authorities involved, in this case the police and social services. It's the only time we ever disclose the private information of any caller. If Kim is as unstable as she sounds, then this child should be taken into care. The only problem was that it would not be possible to do anything unless Kim was prepared to give me her location or mobile number – and I doubted that. Anyway, I decided that Poppy must become as equal a priority to me as Kim, her mother.

"So, Kim, just going back to what you have told me. Buddy is in jail but you have agreed that you will kill yourself and Poppy, and when he finds out he will hang himself. Is that right?"

"Yeah?" she said this in a questionable sort of way. "They will beat up on Buddy every day until he gets the spice that he promised and he can't take it no more, Mister, and he wants to die. My poor Buddy, he wants out of it and he will do himself in when he hears about me doing it."

I wasn't liking her 'poor Buddy' very much. He was prepared to send his girlfriend and his daughter to their deaths on a promise that he would kill himself when he heard of their demise. Sounded a bit of a one-sided pact to me.

"I hope you don't mind me asking this, Kim, but what if Buddy changes his mind?"

"What do you mean?"

"Well, say Buddy hears that you have died and then he doesn't want to die himself."

"Look, Mister, he won't do that … will he?"

"I don't know. Do you really want to die, Kim?"

"Yes. I'm doing it in front of the next train. I promised Buddy and I'm doing it."

"And Poppy too?"

"Well, yeah, of course she has got to come with me."

"She doesn't have to, does she?" I asked.

"What do you mean, Mister?"

"Well, Kim, you can leave Poppy at the station and someone will find her, or you can tell me where you are and I can get social services to pick her up. That way you can jump if you really want to and Poppy can live her life. She is only a baby, isn't she? She hasn't had a life yet, has she?"

I was bricking it because the stakes here were very high indeed and I was praying that another train wouldn't come through any time soon.

"Well, yes, she is only young. But I don't want to die without her."

"Do you really want to die, Kim? You and Poppy, or would you like to spare Poppy and let her make her own decisions when she grows up. Do you think that Poppy will have a better life than you in the future?"

She never had time to answer. I could hear something and I knew Kim could as well. Trains make the tracks vibrate and 'sing' in advance of their arrival. She must have been very standing close to the rails because I could hear this sound, clearly signalling the approach of another train.

"There's another one coming, it's a long way off yet," she reported.

"What will you do, Kim?" I asked as calmly as she appeared to be.

"I'm jumping now," she shouted back.

"Are you going to jump with Poppy, Kim?"

"We have to!" She was screaming the words out now. "It's on its way!"

I could hear the train approaching over the phone. I didn't know where she was, or whether she was on a single rail line or a twin track. I prayed that the train was on the opposite side to where Kim was standing.

"There is a train coming now, can you hear it?"

"I can hear it, Kim."

I was really on a knife-edge, but I said in my calmest voice, "What are you going to do, Kim? Can you tell me?"

"It's what I promised Buddy. I have to jump with Poppy."

I could hear the train approaching fast, sounding louder by the second. I frantically wiped beads of sweat from my forehead.

"You can jump, Kim, it is your decision. But please, answer me this question. Is it Poppy's decision? Is it, Kim? You can put her down and let her live. It will be the best thing that you have ever done."

I knew I was breaking the rules of the organisation by giving advice. But I was thinking then that if anyone else could handle this better than me right now then let them come in here now and fucking do it.

Kim was shouting, "I'm fucking doing it! This is it!"

The train's horn sounded loudly and I could hear the juggernaut getting closer to Kim and Poppy. This was my last chance.

"Do you think that Poppy wants to die, Kim? Have you looked in her face and asked her, Kim? What is she like when you look at her, Kim? Does she smile? Do you love Poppy, Kim?"

The train sounded very close now. Its horn blasted out again, a deafening noise, as though the driver was warning Kim to step back away from his speeding machine.

She screeched out, "I'm …"

Then the thunder of a five-hundred-ton monster drowned out all other sound.

"Kim!" I yelled. "Kim!"

Everything was lost in the din of the train. I heard it speeding by and could almost feel the rush of air. God knows how it felt for Kim and her baby – if they were still alive.

"Kim!" My voice seemed hoarse as I called her name. I was filled with trepidation. "Are you there?"

Sweat was pouring down my face, dripping onto the desk. I looked over at my shift buddy, Libby, who was staring at me open-mouthed; she was probably wondering what on earth I was shouting at. She mouthed the words, "Are you alright?" I gave her a quick thumbs-up to reassure her.

After the explosion of sound everything was quiet on the phone line. After a while, I heard the sound of a baby gurgling. I breathed a massive sigh of relief.

"Kim, are you there?"

"Yeah, I'm here. The fucking thing was too fast for me, Mister," she said, as though trying to excuse herself for failing in her suicide attempt. "They go by so fast; the bloody train is on you before you can jump. I will do the next one."

I was shaking like a leaf.

"You let Poppy live, Kim. How do you feel about that? Do you think you did well?"

"I fucked up, Mister. I just fucked up," she sobbed.

"Listen, Kim. Listen to me, please. You didn't fuck up. You gave Poppy life. You gave her life for the second time. The first time was when she was born. Now you have given her life again. How did you feel when Poppy was born?"

"Well, I was happy, wasn't I?"

"Kim, by not jumping with Poppy in your arms you gave her life again. How do you feel about that?"

"You're trying to trick me now, Mister."

"I'm only asking you to think about it, Kim."

"Well, alright, I'm thinking, Mister."

"I asked you earlier if you thought that there may be a chance that Poppy would have a better life than you, Kim. What do you think, Kim? Could Poppy have a better life than you?"

Kim was sighing. "Oh fuck. She could have, I suppose."

I could hear a heavy diesel engine approaching. At first, I thought, *Oh, shit, another train*, then I realised it was a bus or truck arriving at the station. I made a decision. I was going to try my final gamble.

"Kim, did I just hear a bus arrive at the station?"

"Yeah, Mister, a fucking bus. Why? I ain't getting on it, no way."

"Kim, you can tell me where you are and I can get Poppy picked up by people who will care for her. Or you can go and give her to that bus driver. Or you can both get on that bus together and go home and think a bit more about what you want in life, both for yourself and for Poppy. Is that fair?"

I could hear her sobbing.

"Oh fuck, Mister. I don't know what to do. I promised Buddy. I ..."

I could hear the bus coming to a halt, with the noise of the air brakes and the doors opening.

"What do you want to do, Kim?"

"I don't know. Buddy will go mad."

"Why will Buddy go mad, Kim?"

"Cos I haven't killed myself."

It was one of the craziest things I had ever heard. I took a deep breath.

"Does Buddy love you, Kim?"

"Yeah, of course," she said indignantly.

"Well, if he loves you then he should be really pleased that you and Poppy are still alive. Won't he be pleased, Kim?"

Kim was silent for a few seconds and eventually said, "You don't think that Buddy loves me, Mister, do you?"

"It's not for me to say, Kim, but you need to think about it. Maybe you need to think why a man who loves you would tell you to kill yourself. That's all I'm saying, mate."

After another long silence Kim said, "I'm getting on the bus. You stopped me there, Mister, and I love you for that. Poppy needs to make her own mind up and I need to be there for her."

I almost cried with relief when she said that.

I had to ask her another question. I was nervous to ask, but it had to be done.

"Kim, what will you tell Buddy when he phones you?"

"I shall tell him to fuck off!" she said firmly. "It's not my fault that he got done for drug dealing. I didn't know anything about it. He could have got me and Poppy killed. I just realised, Mister, you made me realise. He could have got us killed. Poor little Poppy."

"You will be alright now, Kim?"

"Yes, Mister, we will both be alright now."

"Well done, Kim. Can you do me a big personal favour? Can you let me hear you get on that bus? Please, Kim."

"Yeah, Mister. I'm getting on now."

I could hear her talking to the driver, and I could tell she was on board from the noise of the engine and the change in background sound.

"I'm on now, Mister."

"That's good, Kim. You phone us if you ever need us okay?"

"Yeah, I will. Thank you, Mister."

I could hear the bus moving off.

"That's okay, Kim. Don't forget we are here for you."

"Oh, Mister?"

"Yes, Kim."

"What's your real name?"

"I'm Robert."

"Thanks, Robert. I won't forget you."

Then she was gone.

I clicked on 'Stop taking calls'. I ran out of the phone room to the toilet and threw up into the pan.

"Fuck!" I gasped. I was mopping at my streaming eyes and running nose with toilet paper. "I'm getting to old for this."

Chapter Thirteen

After washing my mouth out and taking a drink of orange squash, I returned to the phone room. Libby seemed to be busy on a call, in deep conversation and deep in thought. I returned to my place by the window and logged the call regarding Kim and her suicidal thoughts. I then clicked on 'Start taking calls'. The phone, as usual, rang immediately and I answered it.

"Can we help?"

A woman, shrill and very angry, shouted out, "You're a fucking wanker!

"Hello," I replied, "why are you saying that?"

"Because I am saying it. You lot are a bunch of cunts!"

"Okay, why do think that?"

"Cos you are fucking useless and I am going to find you and fucking do you with a knife."

"What's making you feel so angry today, are you able to tell me?"

"You fucking jumped-up piece of shit. Who do you think you are, you're no good for anything!"

"Alright, listen, please. I am going to terminate this call unless you calm down and tell me what it is that is troubling you."

"You, you, fucking scumbag ..."

"I'm terminating the call now unless you stop swearing at me."

"Bollocks."

"Goodbye. Phone back if you have a real problem. Okay?"

Click went the phone line as I cut off the angry woman. This was the Listener's lot. One minute helping a worthwhile cause like Kim and Poppy, the next being subjected to foul-mouthed abuse by a very angry and confused person.

I clicked on 'Stop taking calls' and logged another misuse of service call. This time I recorded it as an abusive call. A bit of an understatement but that was the only option available to me.

Someone once said, "There's nowt so queer as folk." I could not have agreed more.

I looked over at Libby and she was beginning to worry me. Although I could only see her back, she was fidgeting and I could hear her saying, "What do you mean?" It sounded innocent enough but I was becoming concerned. Then she said, "I thought you were genuine. Why are you doing this to me?" I quickly scribbled a note onto a piece of paper and walked over to her, and from the front she looked visibly shaken. I showed her the note, which read, *'Terminate the call if the caller is upsetting you.'*

She nodded to me and told the caller, "That's enough. I am now terminating this call."

She cut off the caller, took off her headset and started to cry her eyes out. I stood there, not sure how to react. With the exception of last week in here with Nicola, I had never laid a hand on a female Listener, especially in this room, alone like we were then. We guys have to be careful these days.

"Are you okay, Libby?"

"He was horrible," she sniffed, wiping at her face. I went into the kitchen and brought her a box of tissues. "Thanks, Robert," she said.

"Libby, why don't we go out of here into the kitchen and I will make us a coffee, and if you feel like it you can tell me about it. Our relief will be here in half-an-hour."

"Yeah, okay," she said, blowing her nose.

Libby opened up to me in the kitchen over our coffee.

"The bloke told me that his wife had just died," she said, more calmly now. "He sounded really upset. He kept saying he missed her, missed the touch of her skin. We talked about bereavement and I even signposted him to those bereavement counsellors, you know."

"Cruse," I said.

"That's it, Robert, Cruse," she said triumphantly.

I was thinking how she seemed like a lovely kid but she sounded all too innocent to me, and this listening business can be a pretty tough world to exist in.

Libby continued, "Then he was asking me if I had nice skin. So I warned him off and he was talking about his wife and I didn't realise it but he was a pervert. I spoke to him for fifty minutes and I didn't realise, and I feel terrible and dirty. At the end he told me that I had been a good girl and he had been playing with himself all through the call and he had just come all over himself and I should be proud. And he thanked me, Robert."

You poor young thing, I thought. She had given up her time to do the intensive training and come here to help people and she was subjected to that cheap perversion on her first solo shift.

"The thing is, Libby, he is sick. He is a vile, horrible man for doing what he did. But he is sick and, in this job, we get them all the time. How are you feeling now?"

"Well, I feel better thanks, but it was horrible. It's because I didn't realise and I felt filthy after it because I was on the phone to him for so long."

"You're not filthy, Libby. You did your best for the caller and when you did realise something wasn't right you terminated him. Talk to the leader about it and he will get you some care from Volunteer Support. Okay."

She smiled. "Yeah, okay."

At the end of the shift, after I had debriefed with the shift leader, I wandered over to The Duck and had a beer. I felt shattered and exhausted. That call with suicidal Kim had really taken it out of me. It was just after seven and I was thinking of picking up some fish and chips and wandering home, but it was raining heavily and the temperature was plummeting. Summer was taking a break. I decided to dial for a pizza when I got home. I was just about to leave and then, out of the corner of my eye, I saw someone I recognised, an Asian girl. Yes, it was Jade, my face-to-face caller. She had returned to haunt me.

She walked towards me. I turned and started to walk away, but she caught me and tugged at my sleeve.

"Why you not speak to me, Robert?"

"Jade, as I explained to you, I am not allowed to meet with anyone I deal with outside of the branch. It's the rules and, more than that, it's the law," I exaggerated.

"Well, it is a stupid law. We can just talk. What harm will it do?"

"Jade, I wish I could but I can't, it's not allowed."

"Who won't allow it?"

"The organisation I work for won't allow it."

"Huh! They won't know," she said, shrugging her shoulders.

I looked at her; she was a very beautiful young woman, dressed the same as she was when I saw her in the branch with a white blouse, tight denim jeans and sandals, with the Jade stone around her neck.

"Jade, it isn't allowed. If anyone from the branch walked in here and saw us together, they would report me and I would be finished. Please understand."

"How will they know who I am?"

"Sorry, what do you mean?"

"How will they know who I am? I could be anybody. Any girl you meet," she stressed as though I was an idiot. "How they know who I am when I only saw you and no one else. Only you I saw and only me you saw. Do you see what I mean, Robert?"

I could understand Jade's point of view, in a way. No one else had seen her in the branch that day. Carl could have done as Jade entered on the CCTV, but he was out of it that morning, lost in his own private world of alcohol and women. The only CCTV record of Jade was when she entered and left the branch, and this would never be looked at, more likely buried in a storage space in the ether net.

"Yes, I understand what you mean, Jade, but it is still not allowed for me to talk with you and it is against the organisation's rules."

"But who would know? Look, just let me buy you one drink as a thank-you for what you did then you go home. Okay?"

I sighed. "Okay."

"Good. What you want, Robert?"

"I will have a glass of pinot grigio, please." I didn't fancy any more lager tonight.

"Okay, you go sit over there and I will bring the drinks." She pointed to a row of empty tables at the back of the room in a private area. I did as she asked, relieved to get out of the main public view. But I still felt very uncomfortable about this situation.

Jade returned with a whole bottle of pinot grigio in an ice bucket. She was smiling at me.

"They tell me that it is cheaper to buy a whole bottle than two large glasses, so here we are."

"Okay, Jade. Thanks."

"Thank you, Robert, for helping me that Sunday. I left you a card, you never phoned me. I guess for the same silly reason you don't want to sit with me now. Yes?"

She poured the wine and passed a very full glass to me.

"Well, Jade, cheers," I said. "I was surprised to get your card, even more surprised that you knew where I lived."

"Cheers," she said. "Why were you surprised that I know where you live?"

"Well, how did you find out where I live, Jade?"

"It's easy, I follow you. People follow each other all the time in Vietnam."

"Oh, I see." I was somewhat surprised at the simplicity of her explanation. "When did you follow me home?"

"Same day as we first meet and after I see you with your girlfriend in here and at station. I follow you then."

"She's not my girlfriend," I said, probably too defensively and too rapidly to hide my true feelings for Nicola.

"She is. I saw you holding hands in here and then kissing outside the station. You look very much in love and she is a very beautiful lady. You look very happy together. She is older than me. Yes?"

I was thinking to myself, *Keep Nicola out of this*. I could sense danger but I did not know from where it would emanate. Even though I was glad to hear that Nicola and I looked happy together, I was determined to keep Nic out of this scenario.

"Well, she is just a friend," I said, now knowing what John the disciple must have felt like when he denied knowing Jesus. To deny what was possibly my love for a beautiful woman like Nicola was a sin. I should be proud and shout it from the rooftops. But, and it was a big but, Jade was dangerous. I could tell.

"Well, you looked in love. Okay," she said finally.

"Jade, can I ask what it is that you want from me?"

"I want to be your friend and be able to talk to you as my friend. You helped me when you did. Why can't you help me now? I cuddle you if you want. I like you, Robert. Why do you no listen to me?"

"Well, that is very nice, Jade. But once I have met you as a Listener, I cannot meet you again anywhere outside of the branch. It's the law. So now we can have this drink and then you and I must part company and not meet again."

She lowered her head and looked very sad.

"But you are the only one who understands me," she said, taking a large gulp of wine. I was dreading the fact that she might start to cry or make a scene.

"Where is your boyfriend tonight, Jade?"

"I don't know. He goes out, I escape. I needed company. I can be with any man in here, Robert, they are all wanting me but, you know what, I don't want them."

"I know you are a very attractive girl, Jade, and I'm old enough to be your father, so let's finish this and I then have to go home because it has been a long day. Okay?"

"In Vietnam old men like young girl, so do old men everywhere. Anyway, I am not young girl, I am twenty-four, I am woman, a woman in my prime is what one man in here say to me."

This young lady seemed so forthright and realistic. With a truly simplistic view on life. She was very different; if she wanted to find out where someone lived, she just followed them, simple as that. How plain and honest is that? I was warming to her but I knew that this was a very dangerous game, full of possible repercussions. My glass was nearly empty and I chinked it against hers as I got up to leave.

"I have to go now, Jade. Thank you for the drink."

"Okay, Robert. Your girlfriend at your house, yes?" she said, smiling, and again, as at the Tube station, I shivered. It was a smile but it wasn't a smile. I didn't like this.

"She is not my girlfriend and she is not at my house, Jade. Try to sort your life out, and I wish you luck."

I smiled at her and turned to find my coat, which I placed over my shoulders and left her, sitting alone. I walked out without a backward glance.

I walked towards my apartment. It was raining very hard and there was a gale blowing, making it very wet, cold and miserable. So different from the recent heatwave. I wondered how the homeless people would cope on a night like this.

I got back home a little bit after 8pm. I live in a three-storey block of apartments; the front entry is on the main road. I live on the first floor, up one flight of stairs, and the garages are at the rear, with a parking space for my Ford Mondeo.

I had ordered a takeaway pizza on the way home and it would be delivered in half-an-hour, so I had time to take a quick shower and change into joggers and T-shirt before it arrived.

Tonight I was feeling lonely. This never normally happened to me but I knew it was because of Nicola. It just didn't seem right to me. We had become close over a period of months and the more I thought about it the more I knew that what happened last week was inevitable. It seemed unfair because we went through all of that and as soon as we reached the moment of closeness, when we actually made love, she took that passion and then immediately left me alone. Now she had delayed her return by even longer and I just was not getting it. I liked to think I loved her, we both enjoyed one another's bodies and now, in her absence, who knew where we were.

She did, however, make it quite clear that she didn't want a serious relationship – and that I could understand. Did she only want a fuck buddy? No, she could get that anywhere, she was a great-looking girl. No, she probably wanted me because of our closeness but, one step at a time, I would just have to wait.

I sat there pondering, when my cat Henry appeared. He was a big ginger and he had arrived from his day's wanderings, gaining entry through the two cat flaps, one in my front door and the door to the flats. Henry was purring and I cuddled up to this ball of fur.

I ate my pizza, leaving a third of it in the kitchen, and it was approaching 10.30pm. I was thinking of turning in when my doorbell rang. I looked out of the window and the rain was absolutely hammering down, so I had trouble seeing anyone or anything. I went out to the apartment door and opened it – but there was no one there. When I looked down the stairs, I could see someone outside the main entrance.

The bad weather had caused it to become dark earlier that night. Switching on the light, I could see a young woman with long black hair. Nicola, I thought at first, and my heart skipped a beat. Then I realised that Nicola didn't have a clue where I lived. I didn't know who this could be. Then I saw the white blouse and denim jeans and I knew who it was.

I opened the door and said, "Jade, what the hell are you doing here?"

Chapter Fourteen

"Oh my God, what has happened to you?" Jade was soaking wet, her hair was matted to her face and her clothes were sticking to her body. She was shivering with cold and, when she looked up at me to speak, I saw blood running out of her nose. The wind and rain had spread the blood over her entire face and there was a small cut with a bruise forming under her right eye.

"Robert, please help me," was all she said before she collapsed half in the door and half out.

I pulled her in and helped her to her feet. Her blouse was torn down the front and she kept trying to hold it together; she was now shivering violently. The jade stone was still in place though.

"Christ, what has happened to you, Jade?" I helped her up the stairs, as I couldn't keep her in the lobby as the neighbours, especially the one on the top floor, would have a field day.

I took her up into my flat and closed the door. She was still shivering violently and sobbing.

"I will get you a towel, Jade. Do you need the paramedics?"

"No, I have suffered worse than this," she replied, breathing heavily. I fetched the towel and wrapped it around her shoulders. I went into the kitchen and came back with a small glass of brandy, which I offered her.

"Drink this. It will calm your nerves."

She drank it in one and coughed and spluttered. She went to wipe her nose with the sodden sleeve of her blouse but decided not to. Water was dripping off her and a damp stain was forming on the carpet where she stood.

Really, I didn't want her here but I couldn't turn her away. I realised I had to help her, in spite of the organisation's laws and rule book. I sat her down in the only armchair in the room, my chair, in front of the television; she was still shivering with the dampness and cold. I realised that she had to get out of the wet clothes and into a hot shower, so I suggested this to her.

"Yes, thank you," she replied.

I showed her to the bathroom and fetched her one of my shirts, a thick lumberjack shirt, which I normally wore during winter. I am more than a foot taller than Jade so it would cover her more than adequately.

I left her to it and went back into the living room. *Oh fuck!* I thought. I could hear the noise of the power shower and, when it stopped, I went to the door and shouted, "Are you okay, Jade?"

"Yes, okay, Robert. I feel better now, thank you," she replied. I went back to my seat and waited, not sure how to handle this.

When she came back into the living room, she was wearing my lumberjack shirt, which reached midway down her calves. She was carrying her own sodden clothes.

"If you have one, can I put these in dryer please, Robert."

"Yes, of course."

I showed her to the kitchen and she put her jeans and blouse and white bra in the dryer. Then she held up the tiniest thong I have ever seen. She held it between her hands and pulled the sides so they stretched and said, "I will put this in too. I just washed this, okay?"

I looked to the floor in embarrassment and signalled her to do as she wished.

"Sorry if I embarrass you, Robert. I don't mean it. I know English men aren't very open to these things. It just normal to me."

I got the feeling that she was teasing me.

"That's okay, let's go back and sit down."

She sat in my number one armchair, my only comfortable chair, and I pulled up a dining room chair and sat next to her. Henry the cat wasted no time and jumped on the chair, nestling into Jade, who started to stroke him. I thought then, maybe misguidedly, that cats get all the luck.

"How are you feeling, Jade?"

"I am warmer now, thank you. I think he broke my nose. John, my partner, I mean."

"What happened, Jade?"

"Well, I went back to the apartment after I finished our wine in the pub and he was there. Someone had phoned him and told me I was in pub with man. He was not happy and he shouted at me, wanting to know who you were. He said he would find you and kill you!"

I felt my stomach heave as she said this so casually.

"Bloody hell! Kill me?"

"Don't worry, Robert, I would not tell him. I just say you were an old friend I once work with and he became very jealous, Robert, and hit me. Not with fist, he hit me with what he calls 'a back hander'. He is very proud of back hander; I never see it coming. He tore at my shirt and I knew he would rape me now, he likes doing that, it turns him on when he is angry through cocaine. He likes to tear my clothes. He throws me on the table and rips my jeans off. He likes to tear my blouse open, pulls my breasts from my bra and bites me. Then he tears my underwear and rapes me, brutally. He is like animal. Anyway, his thumb went in my eye and he cut here." She pointed to her eye. "When he grabbed my hair and tried to force me onto the table, I kick him between the legs hard and I ran out with just these clothes I was wearing and nothing else. So, I have no handbag where I keep my cards and money and passport. He called me a whore and said he would kill me, but I hurt him bad and he does not run after me. It was raining very hard and I have nowhere to go and I come to you, Robert, and I am so sorry."

She reached out and held my legs and rested her head on my thighs and started to shake again and sob uncontrollably. I reluctantly placed my hand on her back and I was trying to comfort her, she was probably in shock. I was very wary of getting close to this beautiful young woman and I really didn't want to hear the sexual detail, but she was an honest girl. Or so I thought then. I had listened to her story with horror and I found myself wondering why she would want to put up with this and I remembered that she had told me that her and this monster were addicted to one another. The chances were she would be back with him tomorrow.

"Would you like some medical attention, Jade?"

"No, I will be okay," she sobbed. "I am so sorry, Robert. I don't mean to bother you with all this crap."

My heart could have melted for her. "That's okay, Jade, don't be sorry. Can I get you some tea, not green tea, I'm afraid, or coffee or cognac or wine?"

"Oh, thank you, maybe wine, please."

I had wine in the fridge because I had bought it in the hope that Nicola would come around. I brought the bottle of Chablis with two glasses and sat next to Jade on the dining room chair.

"Cheers," was all she said; she had stopped sobbing now and seemed normal.

"Cheers," I said. "Jade, why don't you leave this man? He is a monster."

"He will find me and kill me, Robert. I told you and I tell other people, but no one believes me."

"Do you want to be with him, Jade? Really, do you want to be with him? You told me when we first met that he was addicted to you and you to him. Is that really true?"

"It was exciting at first and we had sex that I liked. I have had men in Vietnam when I was a very young girl of twelve.

Don't look so shocked, Robert, it is what happens there, it is the way. I never liked these men. It was very common for girl to have man when she is young, especially twelve years ago. Maybe it is becoming different now but then very normal. Then in university when I come to England, I have one man, an English gentleman, very rich and posh. He wanted to marry me but I don't love him and leave. Then two years without man then I meet John. John was different."

It was the first time she had mentioned his name.

"He was not boring, he was interesting, but it did not take me long to understand that he was a gangster. I sort of loved him and maybe I still do. I will have to go back tomorrow to get my personal belongings and then I must leave him."

"Is John a man with dyed blond hair?"

"Yes, you see him in pub while you were with your girlfriend. Yes?"

"She is not my girlfriend," I insisted. "You will go back to John I think and stay with him. Yes?"

"I don't know, Robert. If I can stay here now, tonight, I will sort things out tomorrow. Is that okay?"

"Yes, Jade, but you must leave tomorrow, do you understand? I will be in big trouble with my organisation."

"Okay, I understand. I think maybe my clothes are dry now."

She got up to retrieve her clothes.

Listening to this, I was amazed she would go back to a brutal thug like her John. It was the second time today that I had heard of such things. I had not forgotten about Kim at the railway station, whose partner, a drug dealer banged up in prison, had told her to take herself and her baby to the railway line and throw themselves in front of a train, and she almost did. *What is wrong with this world today?* I thought.

Jade came back and I poured us two glasses of wine, which emptied the bottle. It was past midnight when I showed her to the spare room, where a bed was always made up for the very rare off-chance that I may have a visitor. She thanked me again and shut the door. I went to my bed.

I was just dozing off, about three-quarters of an hour later, when I heard a quiet knocking at my door. I was almost asleep and I reached for the light switch.

"What is it?" I said rather angrily.

"Please, Robert, let me come in. I'm afraid."

She opened the door and came into my room. She was still wearing my shirt but now it was open down the front, revealing that she was naked underneath except for the Jade stone around her neck and the small white thong I had seen her with earlier.

"Jade, you can't come in here like that," I said in a panicked tone.

"Why not, Robert. Don't you like me?"

She held out her hands, exposing her semi nudity even more.

"I am afraid to be in that room, Robert, it smells damp. Please, I stay here with you tonight. I am afraid to sleep alone in case someone come."

"Oh, for Christ's sake," I said angrily. "Who is coming? Not John?" I asked this in great trepidation; the last thing I needed was that thug turning up here and attacking both me and Jade.

"No, no, don't worry, not him. Anybody it could be, I don't know who, but someone. I am afraid on my own. Let me stay with you."

With that, she dropped the shirt to the floor and stood in front of me with just the Jade stone and thong on. She looked magnificent. Her body was perfectly formed, totally in proportion to her size and she looked like something out of a James Bond film.

I was even more shocked when she jumped onto my bed on top of the covers and said, "You don't have to fuck me, Robert."

I was still wearing my jogging bottoms and T-shirt and I pulled the covers up to my neck, like an old grandad. I was paralysed. Here was a naked woman, one of the most beautiful women I had ever met, getting into my bed and I was paralysed.

She slid under the covers with me, wriggled to the far side of the bed and with her back to me she said with a sigh, "Goodnight, Robert." Within five minutes she was fast asleep.

Part Five

Repercussions

Chapter Fifteen

That night I never slept a wink. I was lying there with a near-naked woman in my bed, who was gently snoring like a little porker. I am a hot-blooded male, albeit a little bit aged, and in the end I left the bedroom and spent the rest of the night in the living room sitting in my chair. I was becoming quite worried. On one hand I knew it was wrong for Jade to be here but, on the other, I didn't know what else I could have done with her. I certainly could not have turned her out into the rain and cold in the state she was in. I thought that surely any member of the organisation would sympathise with me over this dilemma but, then again, I knew that no Listener would have condoned my course of action. I was damned if I did and damned if I didn't.

I finally dozed off at around 5am into a fitful sleep. More than three hours later I awoke with a start and saw the marvellous sight of a semi-nude Jade in front of me. I didn't know what to do at first, then I said quietly, "Jade, please go and cover yourself up."

Obediently, she turned around and disappeared, and then returned to the living room wearing my lumberjack shirt.

I went out to the kitchen to make some tea and when I returned she was curled up in my armchair, looking as though she belonged there. This alarmed me; the last thing I wanted was Jade making herself comfortable. I took the tea over to the dining room table and asked her to join me there.

"What are you going to do, Jade? You do know that you cannot stay here, don't you?"

"Yes, I know," she sighed.

"So, where will you go, Jade?"

"I will have to go back to him to collect my things. Maybe I can stay in a hotel tonight and phone him later to arrange for me to go back, then he may be in good frame of mind."

"Do you have money for a hotel?" I asked, knowing what the answer would be.

"No, of course not. Maybe you can give me some. I pay you back, don't worry," she asked in a matter-of-fact way. I sighed.

"Okay. How much?"

"Two hundred," she said immediately. She held out her hand in expectation.

"I will get it for you," I said and went out to my bedroom to fetch the money, which was rolled up in a sock at the top of my wardrobe. I was again taken aback by Jade's nonchalant manner when I asked her how much cash she needed. It was as though she was used to questions like that.

When I got back to the living room, I was presented with a heavenly vision. Jade was still sitting on the dining room chair, which she had pushed back from the table so that she was more visible. The shirt was unbuttoned and was draped from her shoulders, the whole of the front of her naked body exposed from head to toe. She looked like something out of a porn movie as she laid back in the chair with her legs slightly apart.

"I pay you back now, Robert," she whispered. She was beckoning to me with her hands as she writhed on the chair.

"Jesus," I whispered. I could hardly take my eyes off her and stood there mesmerised by this combined vision of beauty and lust.

"Take it, Robert, you can have me. I don't charge, just take me," she said, breathing heavily.

I was so tempted, so close to grabbing her and holding that sweet body close, but then I came to my senses. I thought first of Nicola, whom I had fallen for big time, and then the organisation, and knew that I couldn't break their code of conduct or the guidelines that had been in place since 1962. We could not have any type of relationship with any caller outside of the branch. That was carved in stone and it was criminally wrong to do so. What had happened with the persistent Jade so far was enough to get me kicked out.

"Jade, you are beautiful and I am flattered that someone like you should offer herself to an old man like me. But I can't do this, for all the reasons which I have explained to you."

She got up from the chair, letting the shirt slip from her shoulders and fall to the floor and she stood in front of me naked, apart from the tiny white thong and the Jade stone around her neck. Her breasts gently moved in synchronisation with her body as she inched towards me.

"Take me," she said, licking her lips. Something inside me spurred me into action and I pushed past her, grabbed the shirt from the floor and threw it at her.

"Cover yourself up and go and get your clothes. You have to leave right now, Jade, sorry, but …" I had no time to finish as her face twisted into a picture of hate.

"Look at me!" she yelled. "I can have any man I want. They all want me because I am who I am and I look like this. You fucking creep, Robert. Are you a fucking queer or what?"

She leapt for me and kicked me between my legs.

"Fuck!" I said as I doubled over and fell to my knees. I tried to get up and, wham, she kicked me again in the chest; it was like a hammer blow and I fell backwards onto my back, propping myself up on my elbows. I am probably one hundred pounds heavier than Jade and a good twelve inches taller but she had put me on my back. These were no ordinary kicks of an angry and hysterical woman but the skilled and precise kicks of a martial arts expert.

She leapt on me and went for my eyes with her long nails. I turned my head away and felt her nails gouge the side of my face. To any onlooker this whole episode would have looked bizarre as I was being attacked by a naked Vietnamese Amazon, but now all thoughts of lust had left me. I just wanted to survive and my massively superior strength saved me as I grabbed her, turned her on her front and pinned one of her arms upwards behind her back until she screamed in pain.

"Calm down, Jade!" I shouted. "For fuck's sake, calm yourself down!"

She was wriggling like an eel and spitting out words of hate until she finally became still and then I could feel her sobbing. I let her go and she got up, picked up the shirt to cover herself, and went to the spare bedroom, grabbing the money off the table as she went. I stood up, struggling to get my breath, the pain in my groin slowly subsiding; fortunately, she had failed to connect directly where it would have really hurt, catching my thigh rather than my testicles.

She came back into the room dressed in the jeans and ripped blouse and carrying the shirt. She fixed me with a glare of pure venom.

"You reject me for that older woman, you must be crazy. She have grey streak in her hair and you rather be with her than take me. You fucking crazy. Your girlfriend is a tart, she fuck other men, I see her with a lot of men, dirty old men want her, she dirty bitch."

Her voice was getting louder and I felt myself losing my cool with her as she slated Nicola. I leapt to Nicola's defence.

"Don't you dare talk about my girlfriend like that, you Vietnamese tart!" I shouted. "Get out and never contact me again. I have told you before: stay away from me. Keep the money and the shirt and just fuck off out of my life forever. You really need help, Jade, you should see a psychiatrist!"

Jade was emanating rage now, especially after I mentioned a psychiatrist. She picked up a wooden carving of an elephant that I had bought in Kenya many years earlier. It was fairly big and heavy, weighing almost three pounds. I thought she was going to throw it at me or batter my brains out with it. But she threw it at the mirror on the wall over the sideboard and it shattered with a noisy crash. She turned to stare at me, breathing heavily, her nostrils flared and she was emitting small particles of spittle from her mouth.

Oh shit, I thought.

I looked at her and said the first thing that came into my head. "That's seven years bad luck to break a mirror."

She turned to leave, throwing the shirt over her shoulders, and as she went through the door she turned and snarled, "Fucking prick, Robert."

Then she smiled that evil smile and said quietly, "I will see you again, Robert."

She turned on her heel and walked out of the living room, slamming the door behind her and I made no effort to follow her. Then I heard the front door slam and looked out of the window to see her striding off up the road, disappearing into the early-morning rain.

It was as though my life had been hit by a hurricane. I slumped down in my armchair and heaved a sigh of relief. I was glad to be alone; even the cat had run off away from the royal battle that had just taken place in this room.

Jade definitely had major problems and I was convinced she needed help. I was worried now also of my status as a Listener. I had, in the last twenty-four hours, not only shared a drink with a caller in a pub but I had invited her into my home, let her use my bathroom to shower and laid in the same bed as her when she was all but naked. I had also given her £200 and had a fight with her. I was probably carrying the scratches of our encounter; I had yet to look in a mirror at my face.

I had broken all the organisation's rules by having contact with a caller outside of the branch. I knew that even though I had avoided actually having sex with her, it made no difference whatsoever. The fact was that I had done what I did for Jade for very charitable reasons but, alas, these things would mean nothing to the powers that be within the Listener's Organisation. If they found out what had happened, I was dead meat, thrown onto the rubbish heap. And God knows what Nicola would think.

Could I have avoided putting myself in this position? Well, Jade was a very different type of individual and she would do anything to get what she wanted; I couldn't think of anything that I could have done to make things turn out differently. But my thinking was from a very selfish viewpoint, as was always the case with me.

I sat there for some time, deep in thought, remembering her parting words, "I will see you again, Robert." I shuddered as I thought of this. I could not get those words out of my mind.

I sat there shivering, then I was suddenly brought to my senses by the text alert tone sounding from my phone. I picked it up. It was Nicola. She was on her way back and should be home by about five, and she couldn't wait to see me.

Chapter Sixteen

I didn't know whether to meet Nicola for a drink or tell her I was out of town on business. I was really worried about the scratch mark on my face, and I wondered what Nicola's reaction would be if and when she saw it. Jade had caught me with two fingernails as she had clawed at me and I had a three-inch-long double scratch mark on my face, as though I had been clawed by a cat. Bingo! That's what I would tell Nicola; she knew I had a mad cat called Henry, so I could blame the scratches on him, poor sod.

I texted Nicola back, suggesting we meet for dinner at an Italian restaurant called La Vella, at the end of the High Street. She replied 'no' because she would feel tired after travelling so far. She suggested I went to hers for a dish of beef stroganoff. It would be easier, if I didn't mind visiting a house that resembled a bank. The address was 43 Balmoral Drive, Welford. Could I get there for 6pm? That did it for me, stroganoff it was. I texted back in acceptance and was very much looking forward to seeing her.

It was now 10.30 and I cleared up the mess of the broken mirror and took a shower and dressed. I made scrambled eggs on toast, which I devoured quickly, and was sitting in my armchair with a coffee when my inner doorbell rang.

Oh, Christ. I hope she's not back, I thought.

It was my neighbour from the penthouse flat above; Commander Charles Dancer RN retired. He was anything but a dancer now, at the age of eighty-nine, and used a series of stairlifts to gain access to his flat. He would often ask me to carry his shopping up the stairs if he saw me. I think he looked upon me as some sort of unpaid man servant, like the valet that he'd probably had in the navy.

It didn't bother me too much as he was a good old character, who still punished the cognac pretty heavily. He stood there in front of me, a short man wearing a brown checked shirt with a tie with a near Windsor knot and yellow waistcoat, cavalry twill trousers and brown brogues. His alcoholic red face had a worried expression.

"Good God, old boy! What has happened to your face?" he said, as I opened the door to him. "Had a fight with a woman, have you? I heard a commotion, sounded as though you and she fell out in a very serious way. Spirited young thing, by the sounds of it. I saw her leave. Nothing like a spirited woman, don't you think, old boy?" I could not have disagreed more with the good commander. Anyway, I did not want to talk about my fight with Jade.

"Yes, Charles, err, morning, how can I help you?"

"I think you had better go down and look at your car, old chap. Someone has let the tyres down."

"Oh no," I said in despair. "What now?"

"Better off without them, old boy. Women, I mean, not tyres. If you have a physical requirement, hire a whore. We used to all the time in the navy, you know, especially in the far east. Singapore, Boogey Street, wonderful whores there. We always had a whore or two on the go, except when the wives were on board, wasn't the done thing then. Oh no, not with the ladies on board," he said, tapping the side of his purple nose with two fingers.

"Yes," I said in total bewilderment at the man's ramblings. "Thank you, Charles. I am grateful to you. I had better go down and take a look."

I left my door open and started down the stairs. I heard the old sea dog shouting after me.

"Better off without them, old chap! Better off, damn it."

I looked back at him as he disappeared around the corner of the landing and I heard the whine of his stairlift taking him back upstairs to his penthouse full of memories.

The garages were on the ground floor at the rear of the block. I never put my car into the garage, just parked it outside in front of the door. I made my way down and there was my car in a very sorry state, with both the driver-side tyres, front and rear, slashed by a knife; it must have been a very sharp knife, but where did Jade get that from? Maybe she carried a knife all the time but she never had a bag or anywhere to conceal it and her jeans were too tight to get a flick-knife in the pocket. I could imagine her with a flick-knife, vicious crazy bitch.

Maybe it was her boyfriend. She had possibly gone back to his place, telling tales about me and he had become jealous. I remembered what she had said about him: "He will kill someone one day."

I shuddered and went back upstairs to search online for tyre companies. I firstly checked the kitchen and a knife was missing; a small but very sharp filleting knife. Jade must have picked this up from the kitchen as she left. I remembered the delay between her leaving the living room and the front door slamming, so she must have slipped into the kitchen and picked up the knife.

"Scheming little bitch," I snarled. There was no way I could involve the police in this so I just decided to get the tyres replaced and put it all down to experience. I needed my car to get to Nicola's that evening.

I spent the rest of the day waiting on a tyre company, who arrived about 3pm to replace my shredded tyres. They did a quick and thorough job for £250. Jade was becoming expensive. I had spent £450 today because of her and I had not even walked through my front door.

I was looking forward to seeing Nicola. She lived in a quiet and upmarket road; Balmoral Drive was in the posh end of Welford. Definitely the stockbroker belt. I thought it best to be discreet and I parked a little way up the road to save Nicola from the eyes and wagging tongues of prying neighbours. I was dressed in jeans, T-shirt and trainers; summer was returning and the weather was quite balmy. I looked like some sort of tradesman who had arrived to give the occupants of number forty-three a quote for work.

I walked to her house, a large detached property with an integral garage, meaning that one of the bedrooms was over the top of the garage. I noticed the mock Tudor woodwork on the top half of the house and thought, *Blimey, I bet Nicola didn't choose that*.

I rang the bell and she threw open the door, beaming her biggest smile at me. She looked wonderful in her baggy cotton trousers and white T-shirt, with her nipples protruding through the material. Her beautiful brown hair was wet from a shower she must have taken.

Then a look of horror came over her as she noticed my face with its scratches.

"Oh God, what happened to you, Robert?"

"Had an argument with my cat," I lied.

"Looks like the cat won," she said. "Anyway, come on in. Welcome to Captain Mainwaring's house."

She laughed as she referred to the TV character in charge of his local Home Guard, who was also the local bank manager. The decor was indeed formal, as the hallway was completely covered in oak panelling, like a bank.

"Come here," she said, grabbing me, kissing me long and hard. My hands were under her T-shirt and she moaned as I massaged her breasts. I moaned as her hand slid down to my groin, where there was significant movement.

We were breathing heavily as she took my hand and said, "Oh, sod the dinner." She led me up the stairs by my hand. We reached the landing and she stopped outside a bedroom door.

"This isn't my room, or David's room, it's a guest room," she said.

We burst in and we were kissing again, tearing at each other's clothes as we collapsed on top of a large double bed, both naked and eager to sample each other to celebrate our reunion.

We stayed in bed until about 9pm when we succumbed to a different kind of hunger. We had satiated ourselves of each other and it was heavenly and beautiful. Nicola was the best thing that had ever happened to me, I knew this for sure now. She was simply wonderful. We pulled our clothes on and went down to the lounge. She had a bottle of shiraz open. I sat on a large sofa and she passed me a large wine glass and sat beside me.

"Let's eat in here on trays," she said enthusiastically. "I'm free now. I can do whatever I want to."

"I think you just did," I said laughing as I pointed up at the ceiling to the bedroom.

We both laughed and she went out to cook the rice, having already made the stroganoff, which was warming through. I sat there thinking how lucky I was to be with a woman like this. But then the black cloud came over me; Jade and her vicious boyfriend. I really wished I had never met that bloody woman. I hoped to hell I had seen the last of her.

Nic came back in with two trays, and then the food and another bottle of shiraz.

"I just looked at the calendar," she said, "and we are on a Listener's shift on Sunday morning at 2am. You had better have your fill of me, and me of you, before then because we can't be doing it in the phone room again, can we?" she asked, giving me one of her wicked grins.

We sat there eating Nicola's wonderful gastronomic creation and I felt completely happy.

We stayed on that sofa until about 1am, talking about everything, and I was getting tired; I had only had a couple of hours sleep last night and Monday night and I realised how complicated the last thirty-six hours had been.

We went to bed and made love again and then slept in each other's arms.

I stayed with Nicola right through Wednesday, when we got up late and went shopping like an old married couple. I had no intention of going home, so I bought a couple of pairs of socks and boxer shorts and after shopping and lunch we went back to hers. Later that evening we cooked dinner and ate and had our fill of each other all through the rest of that glorious day.

On Thursday we got up early and drove in my car down to Brighton. It was a beautifully warm summer's day, one of those mornings when you wanted to sing as the sun warmed you early. We arrived at around 10am and had coffee in a small café. We then spontaneously bought swimming gear and towels and went down to the beach, which was rapidly filling up with people, all hell-bent on enjoying the July sunshine.

I held a towel around Nicola as she changed into a white one-piece swimming costume. I was so tempted to drop the towel at a strategic moment and she squealed in protestation at me daring to do such a thing. She had her revenge though as, when I was screening my modesty under my beach towel, she pulled it away and ran off with it just as I had just drawn my swimming shorts up to my thighs. Her screams of laughter attracted a lot of attention and I am afraid some of our neighbouring beach revellers caught a glimpse of my private bits. I shouted at Nic in mock protest at this outrage.

I chased her into the sea and she looked magnificent in her white swim suit, which showed off her figure beautifully. Splashes of water glistened on her like diamonds in the sunlight. We cavorted in the water and I really wished we were on a secluded beach somewhere else to celebrate her beauty by making love to her there and then.

We stayed on the beach until late afternoon, lying in the sun and taking the occasional dip. I was proud to be seen with a woman who was so physically stunning. It wasn't only that. It was her persona; she could make herself noticed without even trying. People just noticed her; she had a certain charisma and magnetism and I realised, yet again, that I was a very lucky man.

We left the beach and took afternoon tea in the Grand Hotel. We were both not looking our best after a day on the beach, but who cared? We were together as one and we could walk on water.

We arrived back in Welford, picked up a takeaway curry and ate at Nicola's house at the big dining room table. It was so funny; she sat at one end, with me at the other, and we shouted messages of love to each other. We showered together, made love and fell asleep together in the guestroom bed. I didn't want this to end.

I have led an interesting life but those couple of days with Nic were the happiest I have ever been. I was completely besotted with her and I knew she felt the same way about me. If there was a God, he was smiling down on me.

On Thursday evening I had told her I would go home the following morning, if only to feed the cat, who by now would have eaten all the food I had left out for him. I never worried too much about Henry, as I knew that my neighbour, Commander Dancer RN retired, fed him illicit meals.

Nicola and I were due to work together at 2am on the Sunday and she had stuff to do on the Saturday, so we would need to get some sleep before we went on shift. Again, we spent the most blissful Thursday night and fell asleep for a long time.

It was now Friday 7th of July and Nicola didn't have to go to work; the school was in its last week before the long summer holidays and she had been given leave of absence by her very understanding headmaster. I truly hated leaving her that Friday morning and very reluctantly went through my early-morning preparations in slow motion.

Little did I know what would be waiting for me when I returned to my flat.

Chapter Seventeen

I drove home at around 10am through fairly light traffic and parked behind my block. I was reversing back to park as usual in front of the garage door when I spotted it. Someone had sprayed something on my garage door in red paint. I got out of the car and stood staring in disbelief. Halfway up the door, sprayed with a very fine nozzle, was the word in capital letters HYPOCRITE. I stood there in absolute horror. I knew who was responsible – Jade or her boyfriend – and I began to simmer with rage. What had I done to deserve this? I had only tried to help the woman and now I was being stalked by some Vietnamese lunatic, for nothing. I couldn't believe it.

I let myself into the block by the rear door, went up to the first floor and let myself into my apartment. A few pieces of junk mail greeted me and I wandered through to the kitchen to put the kettle on when I noticed that Henry the cat's plate was still full of food and his water was untouched, which was most unlike him, as he was a real old greedy guts. I called him and went to see if he was in the living room. There was no sign of him there, or asleep on my bed, or in the spare room, where Jade had left the bed unmade, with a small dent in the pillow where she had laid her head. God, I wish I could see her head now. I would be very tempted to punch it until there was nothing left of it. After a futile search of the bathroom, I could only assume that Henry was out on the prowl and had probably been doing what I had been doing for the past two days.

I was startled by the door bell ringing. I was becoming on edge. "Fucking Jade!" I cursed.

I thought maybe Jade had called for another fight. I opened the door to be confronted by my neighbour from above, Charles Dancer, dressed immaculately as always in his shirt, tie, waistcoat, cavalry twills and brogues. I had never seen him dressed in anything different.

"Good morning, Charles," I said curtly. I really didn't need this nautical wizard's advice just now.

"Good morning, old boy. How are you? Have you seen your garage door?"

"Yes, Charles, I have. Now I'm really busy at the moment and I have to go," I said as I turned back to retreat into my apartment. Then I had an idea and turned back to Charles.

"When did you notice the door, Charles?"

"Well now, let me see." He was scratching at his chin in an effort to jolt his pickled brain into action and I was beginning to regret asking him the question.

"I was going to the Simpsons for drinks and I went down to get my mobility scooter from the garage. Wretched thing that damned scooter, not like the car, you know."

He had recently written off his car by putting it into first gear instead of reverse and driving it through a wall. He was lucky to get away with it because he was well intoxicated at the time but the investigating police officer was a fellow freemason from the same lodge as Charles. He was now waiting for a new car to arrive. He was still rubbing at his chin when it dawned upon him.

"Ah, drinks with the Simpsons. Thursday afternoon, old boy," he said triumphantly.

Jade or her boyfriend must have done this on Wednesday night when I was out. Maybe she had watched me leave. I found this eerie and worrying and I hoped to God that they had not followed me to Nicola's.

"Okay, thanks, Charles," I said, turning again to go back inside.

"Hang on, old chap," he said, grabbing at my arm. "You need to come upstairs with me."

"What on earth for, Charles?"

"There's a box for you, a parcel. A chap left it for you, a delivery driver, you know, these DP chaps or whatever their company is."

"Oh, okay. Where is it?" I asked, wondering what it could be.

"On my landing, old boy. Up here, come on."

He walked off and sat on his stairlift and I ran up the stairs behind him as his chair, with the usually high-pitched whining noise, conveyed him up to his floor. There, at the top of the landing, was a large cardboard box, with address labels on it and marked for the attention of Robert, no surname.

"I got the delivery chap to bring it up here. I can't lift it and I couldn't bring it inside the apartment because of the smell. Smells like a public convenience," he said dramatically, fanning himself with his hand. He was right; a strong smell of disinfectant was emanating from the box.

"Thank you, Charles." I said, lifting up the box and carrying it downstairs to my place. I had left the door open so I was able to go straight in and I dump it down on a worktop in the kitchen. Charles was right; it did smell of the disinfectant blocks they use in public urinals. The box had a lid to it; it was a large square box. I cut the sticky tape which held the lid in place and lifted the lid.

The box was packed with newspaper mingled with small white blocks of disinfectant material that people hang in their toilet pans or that are used in the pub urinals. It stank to high heaven. When I removed the paper, I could see what the box held. I stepped back in horror and shouted, almost screamed, at the top of my voice, "Oh my God! Fucking bastards!"

The box held my dead cat, Henry. I felt his body; he was stiff as though he had been dead for some time. The knife that had cut his throat was still stuck there and a towel soaked in blood was under it. It was the filleting knife taken from my kitchen on Thursday night – the knife used to slash my tyres.

How could anyone be so bloody spiteful? I was shaking like a leaf; I couldn't believe what was happening to me. Why did that fucking bitch hate me so much and why did she have to take it out on a cat?

I went out to the hallway and closed my front door. The last thing I wanted was Charles coming in giving me his opinions. I sat in my armchair in the living room thinking what I should do. Call the police? Not possible, unless I wanted it known that I had been involved with a caller outside of the branch, the ultimate sin. It would certainly come out if I involved the old bill. Really there was only one thing I could do and that was to track down Jade and her boyfriend, whoever he was, and find out why she was doing this to me.

I was angry enough to want to stick the filleting knife into Jade's body, but I would end up with a long jail sentence, so I decided to let the violence go for now.

First I had to bury Henry. I knew what I would do. There was a shortage of open fields around here in the suburbs of London, so I would take him to my fishing lake and find a quiet spot that I knew of and bury my beautiful old cat there.

It was a forty-five-mile round trip to the lake and back. I wrapped Henry's body in a large tablecloth I had inherited from a very distant relative. I carried him down to the car, then went back to the apartment and picked up the box and its contents and took that down to the car. I kept the knife. I was still thinking of using it on Jade or her bloody bloke.

I went into my garage and found a spray can of black paint and I sprayed over the word HYPOCRITE. I would get the garage door repainted later. I also picked up an old spade.

I drove to the local recycling centre and dumped the box with the newspapers, blood-soaked towel and disinfectant blocks. Then I drove out to the fishery, which was very quiet as usual with perhaps only six anglers using the forty-acre site. I often wondered how they made any money but I knew there was a very big membership and the weather was still not very seasonal, being cloudy and slightly chilly again.

I drove to a very quiet part of the site, thick with trees and bushes, and buried Henry in a thicket there. I was in tears as I buried him; it all seemed such a waste. All that cat had ever given me was love and here he was killed by a cheap-skate drug dealer and his Vietnamese tart.

I drove back into London and headed for Welford. I got myself caught up in the rush-hour. It was gone 6pm by the time I got back. I was looking out for Jade as I drove the streets, searching for her or her boyfriend. There was no sign of either. I dropped my car off at home, walked down the High Street and looked in The Duck. There was no sign of either of them. I knew that Jade, in particular, used this place a lot. By 8pm I was sick of searching.

It had been a pretty sleepless week so far and I needed catch up on some kip. I went back home and sat in the chair and dozed fitfully until 12.30am, when I moved to my bed and slept soundly after shedding a tear for my cat and vowing to take revenge on his murderers. As I lay there, my mind was filled with sadness for my cat and self-pity for the unholy mess I had brought upon myself, together with a deep hatred of Jade. I was determined to find her and have it out with her or her boyfriend. I would not rest until I found them.

The next morning, Saturday, I set out to find her. I left home at about 11am and I searched and searched until the early evening – but there was no sign of either Jade or her bloke. I was really edgy by then and I seemed to be walking around in a trance.

I went home and sat in my chair, festering with silent rage. I didn't feel right, not the same as I normally felt. I was usually bright and cheerful. I should have been that way now, especially as I now had Nicola. Then I realised what was really bugging me. I had become acutely aware of the fact that because of Jade I could lose Nicola altogether for good. But right now, I had to cope with Nicola on a five-hour shift and try to keep all of this from both her and the branch hierarchy.

I noticed something else as well that night. For the first time ever in my life, my right hand had started shaking, not violently but like some old drunk the morning after a heavy boozing session. I put it down to nerves and carried on.

Chapter Eighteen

I arrived at the branch for 1.40am as planned. I went into the kitchen and signed in. Nicola was in there chatting to the two girls we were relieving. They were talking about teaching, a subject in which Nicola was well versed. I mumbled 'hello' to them and went through to the Operations Room. I really could have done without this tonight; I just wanted to go home, alone. Whatever happened, though, I was determined to keep my troubles away from Nicola. I hadn't done a very good job, however, because the first thing she said to me when she came into the room was, "Are you alright, Robert? You seem a little bit preoccupied."

"Ah, yes, Nic, I'm okay, just a bit tired, you know. It was a busy weekend." I smiled.

She came over to me, dressed in a short white summer mini dress and sandals, and I hugged her and kissed her on the lips, then hugged her again for good measure. I really needed that hug and I told her so.

"Why don't you come back with me, Robert, when we finish here in the morning?" she suggested.

I couldn't think of anything I would rather do than to curl up in bed with Nicola after five hours of this place. I thought it ironic that she should ask this because, as a single bloke, working these strange hours that a Listener was obliged to do and then returning home on my own to an empty apartment and an even emptier bed, I had always longed for a female to share those moments of tranquil exhaustion with. Now, here I was with Nicola asking me exactly what I had dreamt of and I was going to refuse her. I had a big problem to sort out, and I fancied my chances of finding Jade and her man on a Sunday.

"Sorry, but I won't be able to, Nic. I have to go to my daughter's to take her to Stansted Airport for a midday flight to Benidorm as soon as we finish here. They are having their first holiday without the children." I hated myself for lying to Nicola but I knew what I had to do when I finished here. I wouldn't rest until I had found Jade and her bloke. I was becoming obsessed.

Nicola looked disappointed and just said, "Oh, okay, no probs. Let's take some calls, shall we?"

I went to my normal place by the window and I logged on, really dreading this wretched phone starting to ring. But I had to be there for the callers and it wasn't their fault that I had fucked up my life. I heard Nicola's phone ring and heard her say, "Can I help you?"

I did the same and no one responded, a SNAP call. Then I did it again and, guess what, another SNAP call. Then another, and another. Someone was fucking about and my patience was wearing thin.

I got up and went to the kitchen, Nicola was busy. I was very tense. I felt as if I was losing the plot with everything. I was worried. I poured a glass of water from the cooler and spilt some of it, my hand was still shaking. I took a deep breath and went back to my work station and clicked on 'Start taking calls'. The phone rang and I answered.

"Can I help?"

It was an elderly man with a deep, monotonous voice. He had just lost his wife of fifty-two years and he droned on about his marriage. He did not want to engage in conversation, he just wanted to preach. I listened to him, all of the time thinking of Jade and Henry the cat. I stared out of the window, looking at the late-night revellers going home and then I saw Jade, walking arm in arm with a well-dressed man, wearing a light-coloured suit, a guy of about my age. Jade was wearing a very short mini dress with shiny things like sequins adorning it. She was laughing – and I was fuming.

The guy hailed a taxi and they both got in, laughing. I saw her drape herself all over him, displaying both buttocks as they slammed the taxi doors and it drove off.

I could not believe I had actually seen her from my window while I was listening to this voice droning on and on. "Of course," he was saying, "life was very different in the sixties, you know. I had been promoted to civil servant, second class, and I had my own assistant. Ethel was over the moon ..."

I could not stand this boring voice any longer and I did something I had never done before: I removed my headset. I scratched my head and looked out of the window again. Did I really see her getting into a taxi with another bloke? Well, fuck me. If I had been on shift with anyone else but Nicola I would have run down into the street and confronted her – and to hell with the consequences. But having Nicola here with me made it impossible to do that.

I looked over towards her, she had finished her call and was staring at me with a puzzled look on her face.

"Are you still on a call, Robert?" she whispered.

"Yes," I replied.

"Where's your headset?"

"Oh, it's here," I said, holding it up.

"Err, sorry to ask, Robert, but why isn't it in the conventional place, like on your head?"

"Ah, yes sorry, umm, I forgot to put it back on after I scratched my head." I placed the headset back on my head and the voice was still there.

"About this time ..." the voice droned.

I gave Nicola the thumbs-up as I turned to look out of the window again thinking seriously about jumping from it. She gave me a bewildered look as the voice in my earpiece droned on.

"Yes, about this time, it was '81, I think. I was promoted again to chief clerk. I had three people working for me then. I remember going home to tell Ethel, and she was so excited. The very next day we booked a celebratory short break down to Eastbourne. Ethel said that I was being reckless but I said, "No, let's do it Ethel, I am the chief clerk now!" And do you know, we threw all caution to the wind and went on a mini break of one night's duration down to Eastbourne. It was during March; I think the weather was clear with a slight warm front, or maybe it was a ridge of high pressure coming in off the Channel. I like the weather forecast, do you? Ethel always watched it …"

I was losing the will to live. I should have tried to get him to the point, but I didn't. I just wanted to pass the time in my miserable state while he rabbitted on. I turned my attention away from the chief clerk and Ethel RIP, and thought of my own massive problem.

Ethel's widower was still talking to me at 3.48am. He had been on the phone for one hour and forty-two minutes and I had only heard a few sentences of what he had said. I sensed he might now be coming to an end of his Ethel-orientated oration.

Finally he said, "Good God, look at the time, it's almost four o'clock. Ethel would berate me for such behaviour and I have to play bowls tomorrow afternoon. There is a lovely lady who has just joined the bowls club, you know, she looks a lot like Ethel. I've already invited her to tea. Well, I must go, thanks for the chat and all that. Don't worry about me, I will call again. Goodbye."

"Bye," I said feebly, as I rang off and clicked on 'Stop taking calls'.

I gave a massive sigh and looked for Nicola but she was absorbed in her own call. I stared out of the window and was simmering about the way I had been treated by Jade. I knew this was eating me up and if I did not sort it out it would destroy me.

After logging the Ethel call, I clicked on 'Start taking calls' and the phone rang immediately.

"Can I help?"

A feeble, insipid male voice spoke to me in a high-pitched tone. "I'm feeling guilty," he said. I know I shouldn't pre-judge but I knew what was coming. I pressed on regardless.

"Can I ask what's making you feel guilty?"

"Well, it's me mum's birthday."

"Good, yes."

"I bought her a present."

"Yes, I understand. You say that you bought your mother a present for her birthday."

"Yes."

"Does that not seem to you like a normal thing to do? You know, buy your mum a present for her birthday."

"Yes, but it's what I bought her."

Oh God, I thought. *Here we go*.

I asked the burning question. "Are you going to tell me what the present was?"

"Yes, I am. It was a basque and fishnet stockings."

"You bought your own mother a basque and fishnet stockings?"

"Yes, it looked lovely on."

"You saw her wearing it?"

"Yes, she lets me watch her wearing her sexy underwear."

"You watched while she was wearing it?"

"Yes, she was in bed with a young boy and he was fucking her. She allows me to watch."

I was growing tired of this pervert, and all the bent people like him. I didn't come here to listen to this shit.

"So, you watched your mother in bed with a young boy. You're a bit of a fucking ponce, aren't you?"

"What did you say?" asked the man, sounding surprised.

"I said you're a fucking ponce and a fucking pervert, aren't you?"

"You can't speak to me like that! You're supposed to listen to me."

"I just have spoken to you like that, shit for brains. Why would anyone want to listen to a lowlife scumbag like you? Why don't you get off this line, you pervert. People like you make me sick. What right have you got to phone this freephone number and speak to us like this."

The feeble voice sounded shocked and hurt to be spoken to in this way.

"I have never been spoken to like this. I was telling you why I felt guilty. I'll report you for this."

"Report me then and I don't want to listen to scum like you ever again. You're a nonce. Fuck off and never phone here again. Ever! Do you hear?"

I cut the caller off. Clicked on 'Stop taking calls' and took my head set off, shouting "Ahhh!"

Waving my arms above my head, I looked over at Nicola, who was staring at me, wide-eyed, in shock. She had probably heard everything. I got up and started pacing the room and then slumped down in the armchair, breathing heavily. Nicola got up out of her chair and stood in front of me. She looked shocked and said, "Oh my God, Robert, what has got into you? I've never heard you speak to a caller like that."

"He was a wanker, Nic, a pervert. Why should they get away with it all the time, pedalling their vile filth to us? Upsetting good Listeners. There was a young girl, Libby, in here the other day, she was a probationary on her first solo shift and this pervert had her on the end of the phone for fifty minutes while he tossed himself off. Libby was so upset that I doubt if she will be back at all because of a filthy little shit like that nonce I just spoke to. I've had enough of them."

A grin spread across her face, then she started to laugh and I looked at her in amazement. She was so gorgeous and I loved her so much at that moment.

"I thought that you sounded a little bit fed-up, Robert."

She was laughing so much it made her fall forward on top of me. She was astride me again, her mini dress rucked up to her hips, and I pulled her towards me. I kissed her and started to undo the buttons on the front of her dress, which fell open exposing her nakedness. My hand reached between her legs and her hands worked on my trousers, my mouth on her breasts. We were going for a repeat performance in the phone room with the good Reverend Moore glaring down from his portrait. He was a 'good Listener' though; he looked neither shocked nor embarrassed today.

We had made love in the chair again. After getting dressed, we went out to the kitchen together to have a coffee.

"It was the funniest thing I've ever heard when you lost it with that pervert, Robert." Nicola was still laughing at that. "I have had two tonight asking me to listen while they wanked off," she continued, "so it is about time the Listeners hit back, even though it was wrong. You or no one else should talk to them like that. Some of them are sick and may need help. But they are like vermin as well and they do get to some of our colleagues. Especially the younger female volunteers, like your buddy Libby. So, on this occasion well done you."

"Well, I'd had enough of them for one day. They are time wasters hogging the lines while some poor soul might be stood on a motorway bridge, someone who really needs us, and that filth is taking up our time and blocking the phone line. I know it's wrong, Nic, but I had enough of it today, so I cracked. Sorry."

"That's okay, but I have been worried about you tonight. You've been a bit distant. Are you sure you are alright, Robert?"

I laughed nervously and said, "Well I wasn't distant when we were in the chair, was I?"

"No, mate, you weren't distant then."

"Good," I said, smiling.

"The thing is though, Robert, as wonderful as it is making love in the chair in the phone room of the Welford branch of the organisation, well, we can't do it any more. We will, I am sure, spend lots of time together and we will make love, I know we will, but we cannot work the 2am shift together any more because the temptation is just too great. We can do the daytime shifts and early-evening shifts when there are lots of people around but this one is taboo. We are here for the callers, not ourselves or our own self-gratification. I hope you see my point of view."

"Yes, mate, of course I do and I agree with you one hundred percent. I shall, in future, do this shift with a bloke or one of the lovely, older, frumpy women. It's your fault anyway."

"Why is it my fault?" she squeaked at me indignantly.

"Cos you're so bloody lovely, that's why." I went over to her and kissed her.

The rest of the shift sped by and I really wanted to go home with Nicola at the end of it but I had a mission to fulfil and I was hell-bent on seeing it through.

I walked her to the station and kissed her before she disappeared into the crowds on her way home to get rest. I was really sad to see her leave, as I knew what I was giving up here. A whole Sunday in bed with Nicola but the simple fact was that I didn't feel like it, not with this Jade thing hanging over me. I had only that dilemma on my mind and I was really feeling strange as a result of her behaviour.

I walked slowly home and went around the rear of the building to check if there was any more damage to my car. Hallelujah, there wasn't. I let myself in the rear entrance and went upstairs locking the front door behind me. I sat in my armchair and fell fast asleep.

Part Six

The Truth Will Always Out!

Chapter Nineteen

I slept in that chair for three hours and was still feeling really tired when I woke up. My right hand was shaking. I put it down to the pressure I was under. I took a shower and dressed in clean clothes. I ate breakfast in a pensive mood and planned my day ahead, mentally listing what I hoped to achieve. Above all else, I had to talk to Jade. I still felt like throttling her but violence would achieve nothing. I needed to corner her or her boyfriend and find out what all this was about. Slashing my tyres, killing my cat, running off with £200 of my money and vandalising my property was not what I deserved. I had only ever helped Jade. I never took advantage of her for my own satisfaction, even when she offered herself to me on a plate whilst she was naked. I had refused her point-blank. Maybe that is what had upset her.

I set out to find her at midday. I walked down to the town centre across the river bridge and turned left into the High Street but there was no sign of her. I knew that she and her bloke spent lots of time in the pubs of Welford, especially The Duck.

I remembered her boasting, "I can have any man I want in that pub; all the men want me because of who I am."

The Duck was busy with the Sunday lunchtime crowd but I did a very thorough search of the pub and there was no sign of either of them. I walked down to the Tube station and waited at the entrance on the off-chance that she may be around. I then looked in two other pubs nearby, to no avail. I went back to the station.

After an hour standing outside that station, I went back to The Duck. I ordered a lager from the bar and, as I turned to search for a place to sit, I saw Jade's boyfriend, John. His dyed blond hair made him stick out like a sore thumb. He was talking to two other blokes, big guys, and I wondered if they were a part of his gang. He saw me staring at him and made excuses to his two companions. They shook hands and John headed my way.

I've never been much of a bar room brawler. I had a couple of good friends who were very good at the art. They were tough and ruthless and they won their fights because they could hit hard and always hit first. Get the first couple of hits in and the fight was won. I never fancied laying into someone like that. I would rather do it from behind with a stranglehold so that you cut off the flow of blood to the brain by rendering your opponent unconscious, or by hitting the bastard with a bar stool, again from behind. Far more practical to do it that way.

John was heading straight for me and I grasped my pint glass tightly, half in fear and half to use as a weapon. He was a few inches taller than me, well built, wearing a leather jacket over his T-shirt, with jeans and trainers. No boots to worry about, I thought. His face was slightly spotty and red, drugs I thought, his dyed hair sticking up all spiky. He was an ugly individual.

"Relax, mate," he said as he sauntered up to me with his right hand held out. I grasped it. "I'm John, and I think that me and you better have a chat." He spoke in a broad East End accent.

"Yes," I replied. "I think we better had. I'm Robert, by the way.

"I know." He pointed to a table at the back of the bar. "Over there."

He seemed very sure of himself, but I suppose I would have been too if I was a gang leader with two heavies watching over me.

We sat down. He was drinking what looked like Coke, but was probably laced with rum or vodka.

"Anything that you want to know about Jade, ask me now and let's get this over with. But one thing (he pronounced thing like fing) you need to know is that I ain't what she makes me out to be. Alright?"

"What do you mean, John?" I asked, relieved that I wasn't rolling around on the floor having the shit kicked out of me.

"Well, I suppose Jade has told you I'm an awful person. A drug dealer, I bet. A gangster. Yes?"

"Err, yes."

"That I beat her up and raped her. Yes?"

"Yes."

"She's told you that I am big in the underworld and that I have people done over for crossing me. Yes?"

"Yes, mate, she did," I was beginning to see Jade's story unravel.

"And those two geezers over there, the ones I was talking to, I suppose you think that they are my minders, gangsters too?"

"From what I've been told I did draw that conclusion. Yes."

"Well, you're fucking wrong, mate. They are plumbers."

"Plumbers?" I was astounded. I didn't expect them to be plumbers.

"Yeah, plumbers, same as me. I got my own business with two vans on the road. In August I'm getting a third van. Those two…" he pointed at the two guys, "they are coming to join me, to work for me. I just landed a big contract on that estate they're building down in Farnham. One hundred and thirty starter homes, hundreds more to come. I'll have forty vans out on the road before I'm finished."

I shook my head in disbelief. Jade had been so convincing in her account of this man. "It's not the same as I was told. Sorry," I said.

"And, just for the record, the nearest I get to drugs is a quick spliff of a Saturday night when I'm with Jade or my mates. That's it, mate. I ain't got time to snort that shit." He held up his drink. "This ..." he said, swirling the dark liquid around in the glass, "this is Coke. I ain't got time to drink alcohol either. I'm teetotal, mate. Sorry to disappoint you."

I looked down at the table, dejected. "Oh," was all I could say.

"Look, mate, what's your name, Robert ain't it? Look, Robert, Jade is a compulsive liar, she is totally incapable of telling the truth. Lies about everything, she is bloody mental, mate. What did she tell you that she did for a living?"

"Err, computers, a programmer, no a systems analyst for Barclays."

He laughed out loud, throwing his head back.

"Systems analyst, my arse. She's a hooker, you know, a prostitute, an international prostitute and a very upmarket one, mate, believe me."

I remembered then about Tuesday morning in my apartment when she was draped naked over my chair telling me, "I won't charge you, take me now."

"Oh God," I said. "I believed everything she told me. How did you get involved with her?"

"I met her in here a year ago. Couldn't believe my luck. She is fucking gorgeous, ain't she? I thought I had cracked it. She moved in with me within a week and then it all started, fucking trouble, mate. But she is the best shag I ever had and a body to die for. She caused me loads of trouble, she was always attacking me if she couldn't get her own way and the police were regular visitors to my gaff. She used to keep disappearing for days at a time and then come back and, in the end, I put up with it purely for the sex. Mind you we did click there; she was really into it as well but she was still flogging herself all around London. She came to see you in the Listening thingy to talk about her childhood.

"She was abused at the age of twelve by her uncle and then they put her on the game, flogging her to Eastern

European paedophiles. She had a terrible life and she hates white men, apart from me, that is. She has a vendetta against all western men, it doesn't matter what nationality, and you have probably upset her in the opposite way by the very fact that you have rejected her. She doesn't know what she is doing when the red mist descends. She will kill some fucker one day, believe me. She might have done so anyway. I am sure you will see her again at some stage, full of apologies. I last saw her a week ago, she has met some Dutch fucker who works for Royal Dutch Shell Oil. He is minted, mate, and they are going to live in Holland, they leave today from Heathrow. They were out on the town last night. He came in here with her and even bought me a drink, the cheeky bastard. I took a bottle of Bollinger off him; I didn't drink it though. She'll be back, wait and see. I will give her a week with him and it will all kick off and she will take a load of money from him and back she will trot to John boy. Are you all right, Robert?"

I was reeling from all of this. "Yes. What happened to her on Monday night, her face?"

"We had a rare up about the Dutch twat and she went for me again. She's into Kung Fu or something and she bloody hurts when she kicks. Her blouse did get torn before I shoved her away, probably a bit too hard, and she fell over the back of the sofa and hit her face on the coffee table. That's God's honest truth. I suppose she told you I beat her up and raped her on the table."

I nodded silently. I was like a zombie. I was stunned by these revelations. I mumbled, "Yes, she did say that."

"I knew she would. It was her fantasy, she loved acting that scenario out, she got off on it. She would even make me tear her clothes, she loved it. The thing is, Robert, she loves anything to do with sex, she is definitely a nymphomaniac and she also earns a lot of money from it. On Monday night though, she whacked her face and ran off and came back the next day, and that's the truth!"

"She is leaving today though," I said. "That's one good thing, we can have peace. For a while, anyway."

John gave me a very strange look.

"I wouldn't bank on it, Robert, cos, before she left, she posted a letter to the head honcho Listening bloke, or whatever you call him, complaining about you. I told her she was stupid and that was taking it too far but she sent it anyway. I don't know what happened between you two, only that you turned her down. Fair one, mate. I don't want to know what else went on but she ain't half got the hump with you. Killed your cat, yeah?"

"Yes, she did." I said, completely in a daze, I was so shocked at all of this and now the news of the organisation being told was the final nail. I sighed. "Oh God."

"I doubt if he will fucking help you, mate," John said. He pulled out his wallet and produced a business card. "I'm going to leave you now, Robert. I got to get back to my plumbing. See, I even work on a Sunday, mate. I expect you have a lot to think about. Take my card, it's got my mobile number on it. If I can be of help give me a call, okay?" He offered his hand; I weakly took it and he was gone.

I was dumbfounded. Jade had sucked me in good and proper and now I would be thrown out of the Listening Organisation. Then Nicola would find out. What would she say about it, especially as I had told her a load of lies to cover up the Jade episode.

I was dead meat, whichever way you looked at it. I held out my right hand and it was shaking. Jade was having a very bad effect on my nerves. My whole demeanour felt heavy; it was hard work to move my eyelids. I wanted to break down and cry. I sat there for a long time contemplating what I should do. If the letter had not arrived at the Listening branch over the weekend then it definitely would by tomorrow and Ryan, the branch chairman, was in there every day. I would be called in and given the chop as soon as he read the letter and there was nothing I could do about it. Oh shit. I decided I would have to tell Nicola straight away, face to face. I picked up my mobile phone to call her.

Chapter Twenty

I was in a very nervous state as I drove to Nicola's house. I had fallen head over heels in love with her and I was desperate to save our relationship. I rang her door bell and she bounced to the door, laughing.

"I knew you couldn't stay away," she said, grabbing me and kissing me on the lips. She was wearing a simple light blue summer dress and I wished, at that moment, that I was dead because I knew that what I was about to say would hurt her.

We sat on a sofa in her living room and I told her the whole sorry saga about Jade, from when I first met her as a face-to-face caller to meeting her boyfriend, or ex-boyfriend, a few hours earlier. She listened in complete silence; I was talking to a Listener, someone who is used to listening without interrupting.

When I finished, we sat in silence for a while. I could see this had bothered her very much. Her face looked drawn and in pain, her normally bright and sparkling eyes were grey and dull. I felt like a treacherous dog, my whole body and mind had turned numb. She finally broke the silence.

"When you saw her the first time, in the branch, on the face-to-face, and she asked you to meet her, why didn't you report it to your shift leader?"

"Well, I, err, I have told you many times in the past that I don't like debriefing and, in particular, I found, Bryn, who was leading that morning, very difficult to talk to and then, of course, I didn't want to open up a can of worms."

"Oh, Robert, you have definitely opened up a can of worms, be in no doubt about that. Was the reason for not telling the leader about her suggestion that you both meet for a drink, because you actually wanted to see this very attractive young woman again?"

"No, no, Nic, not at all. I didn't want to see her again."

"When she left you the card at your home, why didn't you bring it into the branch and show it to one of the committee members?"

"Because I ripped it up."

"It's what you call destroying the evidence, Robert."

I tried to argue with her, but she raised her hand and I shut up. "When you saw her in The Duck last Monday, why did you bother with her? Why didn't you just leave?"

"Well, I thought it best to talk."

"Maybe you wanted to do more than talk to the Vietnamese whore," she said, with rancour and bitterness.

"No, not at all. I told her this wasn't allowed as a Listener, that I couldn't do this."

"But you still finished off a bottle of wine together. Yes?"

"Yes." I was on the point of giving up as Nicola's logical arguments were overwhelming.

"When she arrived at your apartment, why did you let her in?"

"Well, it was raining. She was wet and cold, she was shivering, whether with the cold or with shock, I didn't know, and her face was covered in blood. What else could I do?"

"The next morning you gave her £200 for a hotel, knowing that under the rules of the organisation you were not meant to be with her. Why didn't you call a taxi and send her to a hotel that night as soon as she arrived at your house, and then phone Ryan at the branch and tell him all about it."

"I didn't think."

"No, you didn't, did you? Are you sure that you didn't fancy a bit of this gorgeous woman? She didn't take long to get her kit off, did she?"

"Her clothes were wet through, she was shaking with cold and she couldn't stay in wet clothes, Nic. Come on?" I pleaded for some understanding, but none was forthcoming.

"Did she look good naked, Robert? Did you like a young chick flaunting it in front of you? Eh?"

"I didn't know what to do, Nic. I fucked up."

"Yes, but you laid in bed with her, didn't you, eh? You laid in bed with a twenty-something girl who was completely naked apart from a thong and you even told me that she resembled a porn star. Fucking hell, Robert!" She was almost in tears at this stage. Her fists were clenched and her face was red with rage.

What have I done? I thought.

"I didn't stay in the bed, I slept in the chair. I didn't touch her, Nic, honestly." I was pleading with her now. But she was not listening to my pathetic excuses.

"Why have you lied to me, Robert? She assaulted you the next day, she murdered your cat, she slashed your tyres and vandalised your garage. Why didn't you phone the police?"

"I thought it would upset everyone. I thought it would upset you."

"Oh, you have definitely upset me, Robert. But what has really upset me is your lies and how easy it is for you to lie. The scratch marks on your face, you blamed your bloody cat for them and I fucking well believed you, like the bloody idiot that I am. Do you know that earlier this morning I wanted so much for you to come back here with me so that we could be together after our shift? And you lied about taking your daughter to Stansted. You lied so easily; you are very good at lying, Robert. Aren't you?"

"I didn't mean to lie. I …" I couldn't think of anything else to say. I had lied and that was that, there were no excuses.

"I spent eleven years listening to my husband lie to me, Robert, and I fell for every lie he mouthed at me. He had affair, after affair, after affair, I know that now. I was a mug." She looked so sad.

"And here I am now starting a relationship with a man I love and you started lying to me as soon as our relationship had started." Tears were running down her face. "Oh yes, Robert, I love you and you have lied to me already. My mother warned me against getting involved with you so soon after I had finished things with my husband. She said that I didn't know you and I said that of course I knew you. I had worked with you in the Listeners and you were wonderful. And do you know what good old Mum said? She said that anyone would sound lovely if they were talking on the phone to vulnerable people as a Listener. She said that you are all lovely people in that place, and she warned me to be careful, to tread carefully, until I got to really know you. Well I know you now, don't I? You are a fucking scheming liar, Robert."

I could feel this conversation was coming to an end and it didn't look good for me and her. I couldn't blame her. I had completely messed this whole Jade episode up. Everything I had done was the wrong thing. I turned to her and held up my hands and pleaded.

"Nic, I am so sorry. I don't know what else to say. I know that I have hurt you and I didn't mean to, please, Nic."

"Oh, you have hurt me, Robert, and let us be absolutely clear, it isn't the fact that you entertained a naked woman in your apartment, not that at all, it is the fact that you lied to me, Robert. You deliberately lied, and that I cannot forgive."

She stood up before I had a chance to respond and pointed to the door.

"Sorry, but I can't do the lies any more, Robert. You had better go."

"Oh, Nic, I love you," I said pathetically, fighting back my tears.

"Well you have a very strange way of showing it."

She went to the front door and opened it for me. She waved me out as though she was directing traffic and never said another word as she gently closed the door behind me.

I went out and sat in my car. I was more miserable than at any other time in my life. Nicola had not only verbally destroyed me, she had made me realise what a prat I had been and now I had lost her. Lost the woman I loved. My hand was shaking and my whole body started to tremble.

I drove home slowly and I let myself in the back entrance. When I got up to the kitchen, I opened a bottle of pinot grigio and drank the lot, followed by a bottle of shiraz. I didn't give a toss about mixing red and white, I just wanted to blot everything out. I finished off with a half bottle of brandy, went up to bed, collapsed fully clothed on top of the duvet and slept in a drunken coma until 8am the following morning, when I woke with the mother and son of all hangovers.

I struggled to the bathroom, showered and changed and just sat in my chair in the living room, my heart broken. I had only just got so close to Nicola and now, what a few days ago seemed like such a solid loving relationship, was a wreck. I vowed that when I got over this and had got myself back to normal, I would have nothing more to do with women, ever. The trouble was, though, I knew that I would never get over a woman like Nicola.

My phone rang at 11.30am. It was Ryan, the branch chairman. He told me he had received a letter from a caller making serious allegations about me and could I attend the branch that afternoon at 4.30 for a meeting with him and another couple of members of the branch management committee.

I asked no questions, nor did I offer any explanation over the phone, I simply told him I would be there.

Chapter Twenty-One

The hours dragged by until it was time to leave for my meeting with Ryan at the branch. I had sat in my living room all day, drinking coffee and just thinking of what I had lost with Nicola and whether there was any way back for us. I knew the answer was a resounding 'no'. Nicola had made it clear that she could not tolerate lies in a relationship, and I had crossed the line and paid the price.

I walked to the branch in the warm July sunshine, it should have felt good to be alive but it wasn't. In town I stood on the river bridge and looked down at the slowly flowing river. I wondered what it might be like to jump into the river and let it take me, to swallow me up, to sink into its dark depths and be unable to see the ugliness that was on earth; to be deafened to the noises that dominated my life and numbed from the pain that was my life.

It seemed very tempting to jump and to find peace. I stood for some time, staring at the river. Then I looked at my watch: 4.30pm. I had to move on.

I let myself into the branch using the key pad codes, as I had done hundreds of times before. I climbed the three flights of stairs that led to the general office. I passed the lobby that led to the kitchen and the Telephone Room and I knew there would be two volunteers in there listening to the world's troubles, listening to someone else's world, in the never-ending listening vigil.

I stood outside the office door and took a deep breath. I knocked once and entered. Ryan was sitting behind the large desk. A big man with handsome features and silver hair, he was Ryan 1028 – and that was all that I knew about him. We didn't delve into each other's past or present as volunteers, we just got on with the job.

Sitting in a high-backed office chair to the right-hand side of the desk was Brenda. She was on the committee and was also my leader when I took the Tonia call. Brenda resembled what I imagined a 1930s schoolmarm would be, but in her sixties now, her brown hair tied up in a bun on top of her head and a brown cardigan over her white blouse and a tweed skirt. Her spectacles were perched on the end of her nose.

Sitting in another high-backed office chair to Ryan's left was the third member of the jury. It was Bryn, who had led my shift on the day that Jade had called into the branch. He was not a member of the committee but was obviously a key witness. It was odd because Bryn had a deep, loud Welsh voice that boomed to you when he spoke but he was only a very slightly built man. He was so small that only the top part of his chest and his head and shoulders were visible as he sat behind Ryan's very large desk. I thought he resembled a ventriloquist's dummy, slumped in the chair waiting to be lifted up and sat upon Ryan's knee before speaking. It was odd that such a loud trumpeting sound could emanate from such a slight and fragile frame. He was a retired manager from the National Coal Board and probably had never done a hard day's work in his life. These were the triumvirate who would decide my fate and I already knew what the verdict would be. Guilty as hell.

"Take a seat, Robert," Ryan said, gesturing to the only seat available, a wooden hard-backed chair similar to the ones you saw in the war films when the Gestapo caught a member of the French resistance and tied them to a chair before pulling their teeth out.

"You know Brenda and Bryn," he said, taking it for granted that I did. I mumbled a response that I did know them, sort of.

Brenda and Bryn were both looking at me as though I had carried a bad smell into the room. Ryan held up a letter. I could see the small delicate writing in blue ink on the paper and I knew it was Jade's script.

Ryan coughed and said, "This letter is from a young lady named Jade who called in here on Sunday the 29th June and saw you in a face-to-face meeting. We have looked back at the CCTV and can confirm that you let her into the branch and that you let her out again, so there is proof that you interviewed her on that date." *Why did they need proof*, I wondered?

"At that time, Bryn was leading the shift," Ryan stated.

"I was," boomed out Bryn's voice. I almost smiled as I thought that Bryn should have added "Me laud" to the answer, as though he was in court, which the stupid sod probably thought he was.

Ryan continued, "You phoned Bryn before you took the face-to-face meeting with Jade, is that correct?"

"He did," interjected Bryn.

Ryan nodded at Bryn. "Thank you, Bryn. Now, Robert, Jade tells us in her letter that she came to the Listeners because of problems in her relationship with her boyfriend John."

"He told me that," confirmed Bryn, speaking as though I wasn't there.

"Yes, she mentioned her relationship," I said.

"She also told you that the reason for the problems with her relationship was her battle to get herself out of prostitution, which she had been involved in since she was a young teenager in Vietnam."

I was horrified at this; she was lying.

"No," I said. "She didn't mention that she was a prostitute, she told me that she was a systems analyst with Barclays Bank and her partner was a drug dealer who beat her and raped her and controlled her. The boyfriend was her main problem."

"He didn't tell me that she was a prostitute. Dew, dew," interjected Bryn, whilst swearing discreetly in Welsh.

"She never told me she was a prostitute, that's why I didn't tell you! You bloody knob!" I shouted at Bryn. I was becoming very frustrated by both the lies and Bryn and his constant chipping in.

"Knob, he called me. Bloody knob. Did you hear that? Sorry for swearing, Brenda." Bryn was perplexed. I didn't know whether he had ever been spoken to like that before.

Ryan looked at me sternly. "Robert, please refrain from using insults. There is no need for it."

"No need for it. Knob he called me," repeated Bryn.

"Sorry, Ryan, Bryn, Brenda." I looked at them each in turn as I apologised.

Ryan continued, "Jade the caller says that while you were sat with her you kept looking at her breasts and made lewd comments about a necklace she was wearing."

Brenda wriggled in her seat. "Oh, my God," she said, looking upwards as though to find a heavenly presence to strike this sinner down with divine retribution.

"That's a lie," I protested.

"He didn't mention a necklace to me. Nor her breasts. Sorry, Brenda," said Bryn.

"So, you didn't mention her necklace at all?" Ryan asked.

"Well, I did. It was a Jade stone. I didn't know at the time, so I asked what it was."

"Really," said Brenda, fidgeting in her seat again.

"Jade says that you asked her out for a drink."

"He should have reported that to me. Asked her for a drink. Well, well." Bryn sounded offended.

"I did not ask her out for a drink. She asked me," I said in a submissive way that betrayed my disinterest in these proceedings, as I well knew what the outcome would be.

"She asked you out for a drink, you say," asked Ryan.

"Yes."

"Did you report that to Bryn at your debriefing?"

"No, he bloody didn't," said Bryn, adding, "Sorry, Brenda."

"No, I didn't report it." I was losing the will to argue my case by now.

"You should have reported it, Robert," said Brenda.

"He didn't tell me," said Bryn, shaking his head.

"She was pursuing me and followed me home at some stage to find out my address and a day later she posted a card with her phone number on it through my letterbox asking me to contact her urgently so that we could meet up." I was desperate to make them understand that Jade was the one doing the chasing, and not me.

"A card?" repeated Ryan.

"Through your letterbox?" repeated Bryn.

"Where is the card, Robert?"

"Well, I don't have it with me." I realised that I had probably dropped myself further in the mire by bringing this up.

"Okay," said Ryan, like a headmaster coaxing a wayward pupil to confess their sins. "Where is the card now?"

"I tore it up and threw it in the bin." I blurted out the answer knowing that I was done for anyway.

"Destroyed the evidence!" shouted Bryn. He had drawn much the same conclusion as Nicola had.

"Stupid," said Brenda, shaking her head.

Ryan agreed with Brenda. "It was stupid. And did you tell anyone in a senior position in this branch about this card, Robert?"

"No," I confessed like a condemned man.

"Well, you should have," snapped Brenda.

"Indeed," agreed Bryn.

Ryan continued to read out the damning evidence. "Jade says that she saw you in the local pub later that afternoon and you kept staring at her, even though you were with a girlfriend. She says that you often went into that pub looking for her and that you finally caught up with her last Monday, a week ago today, and you bought her a bottle of wine and you shared an intimate drink together."

"She bought it. Oh, what's the point!" I raised my hands in the air in a gesture of futility. I was ready to hoist the white flag.

Ryan looked annoyed. "The next allegation is very serious indeed, Robert, so there is every point in us pursuing this. Jade the caller says that later that night she arrived at your house after arguing with her boyfriend and you invited her inside and then told her to go and take a shower. After taking the shower you gave her one of your shirts to wear and she wore this because you took her clothes away from her and she was forced to wear the shirt with no other clothing underneath the shirt."

Brenda looked fit to burst. "Really," she said, "it's disgusting."

Bryn was shaking his head. "I can't believe it," he said.

I tried to make my point but I felt it would be lost on them.

"She arrived at my flat wet and cold and shivering. It was a cold and rainy night; she was bleeding all over her face and I offered her a hot shower and a thick large shirt to wear while her clothing was drying in the tumble dryer."

It was a waste of time in me saying anything. They just stared at me in disbelief.

Ryan picked up the letter again. "Jade says that after giving her a lot of drink you then went to bed and invited her to join you and she got in bed with you while she was wearing a small thong and nothing else."

Bryn looked puzzled. "What's a thong then?"

Ryan explained. "It's a piece of modern female underwear."

He turned his gaze away from the terribly perplexed Bryn back to me.

"Jade says that apart from this one item, she was completely naked in your bed while you were also in that bed."

"Well I have never heard ..." Brenda was very agitated now, wriggling and squirming on her chair, horrified at the revelations of blatant pornography.

Bryn was still puzzled. "Naked, was she? What about the thong then?" He looked from Ryan to Brenda, then he averted his stare to me, his eyes pleading me to reveal more details of my encounter.

Ryan looked very stern indeed. "Robert, were you in the same bed as this naked woman? Yes or no, Robert, answer me."

I lowered my head. "Yes, I was."

"Really!" gasped Brenda. "A caller, she was a caller."

"He has admitted it," said Bryn, in a triumphant tone. "Admitted it!"

Ryan was staring at the letter with a frown on his face. "She says that the next morning, after a fight with you in which you both cavorted around on the floor again whilst she was still naked, you returned her clothes and she managed to escape. Before she left you offered her a payment of £200 as settlement for services rendered. She says she will not involve the police but thinks that we Listeners should know what type of person we have working for us."

Ryan looked as though he had finished this unjust and comprehensive condemnation of me.

"She assaulted me," I protested. "She vandalised my living room, stole £200 from me, murdered my cat, slashed the tyres on my car and sprayed red paint on my garage door. And now she has told a string of lies and exaggerations about me."

"Well, well, I have never heard anything like it. Cavorting, naked," summed up Bryn.

"Filth," said Brenda.

"Guilty," said Ryan.

"Oh, shit," I said.

Ryan now only needed to don a black cap, as judges used to when they pronounced the death sentence on murderers. He calmly said, "Robert, you have broken the most important rule that we have to abide by. You have had dealings with a caller outside of the branch. That is bad enough but you also chose to imbibe that caller with alcohol in a public house. You then invited her into your home and slept in a bed with her while she was naked and then cavorted with her again while she was naked on the floor of your living room. The sexual conurbations I do not wish to discuss.

"You also deliberately kept this series of events from your fellow Listeners and the committee of this branch. What you have had the good grace to admit to is bad enough, it is what you haven't admitted to that I find disturbing. You are not a fit and proper person to deal with vulnerable people and therefore you are relieved of your duties as a Listening Volunteer at the Welford Branch. You must never enter this building again. The pass codes on the key pad locks will be changed within the next half-an-hour. Your photo will be removed from the volunteer's gallery and you will be listed as a leaver. No explanation will be offered as to your reasons for leaving, Robert. Prior to this episode, as far as we all know, you have been an excellent volunteer and you have helped a lot of people through very difficult times, and I thank you for that. What you have done with this caller though, Robert, is unforgivable. You can go now and I can only wish you good luck for the future."

The three of them looked very sad as I left the branch for the last time and so was I, very sad indeed.

Part Seven

End Game

Chapter Twenty-Two

I left the branch with a heavy heart and I felt very hard done by. Yes, I could see that I had breached the rules by having a drink with Jade and by allowing her into my house and for not reporting these incidents. But, bloody hell, she had really laid it on thick in that letter and had done a perfect hatchet job on me. I was perplexed as to what had driven her to be so spiteful. I was dumbfounded. It had been the worse twenty-four hours of my life. Dumped by Nicola and now sacked from the organisation, the two things that I truly loved in life, both gone.

I headed for The Duck and booze. Before I went in, I turned and looked up at the building and the window that I used to look through, down on the world below. Well, I wouldn't be doing that again.

The pub was packed with early-evening drinkers. I found a space at the bar and stood there, ordered a pint of lager and knocked it back in one. Then I ordered another, then another. I was still there at 8pm and had finished five pints of the stuff and was just ordering my sixth when I felt a tap on my shoulder. It was John the plumber, Jade's ex.

"Hello, Robert, how's it going?" he asked. I looked at him, feeling a bit drunk.

"Great, John. Yesterday my girlfriend dumped me and this afternoon I was thrown out of the Listener's Organisation. Couldn't be better, mate. Jade has done a bloody good job on me, I can tell you."

"Oh, mate, I'm so sorry. Jade is a fucking bitch. She's fed up with that Dutch bloke already and she is intending on coming back in a week's time when she gets some money out of him. She says he smells. Something about his breath. She texted me earlier. She always comes back to me," he said, rather triumphantly.

"I wanna see her, John. I need her to put these things right with my girlfriend and with the Listeners. She has fucking well destroyed me, messed my life up real proper, and I don't know why because I never laid a hand on her. Never."

"I believe you, mate. She has got a personal vendetta against all white men because she blames them for what she is today. That Dutch guy is about to find out the hard way as well. She is telling me that she's going to get treatment when she comes back and that we can be together forever. Like a mug, I'm sort of believing her."

I was beginning to understand now that he had put it like that.

"Can you get her to come and see me, John?" I said. "I will go down on my knees and beg her to put these things right, mate, honest I would."

"I will try, Robert. I will be trying like hell to get her to go for treatment from a head shrink too, cos she needs it. She really does."

"Good luck with that, John." I said with a certain amount of irony.

"Yeah, Robert, I need luck. I know, mate, that she definitely does need to make amends big time for what she has done to you. It is fucking outrageous. I will try to talk to her as soon as I can but it's probably a case of waiting for her to come back here. That's all I can suggest. Give me your mobile number, mate. Ring the number on the card I gave you yesterday then I will have yours, okay. You've still got it, haven't you?"

"Yes, it's in here," I said, fishing my wallet out of my trousers.

We logged each other's numbers on our phones and I looked up at this guy who I had heard so many bad and dreadful things about and said, "Thanks, John, and sorry I thought badly of you. You're a good egg, mate."

"Yeah, thanks, Robert, it's a shame Jade cocked things up for you. She messed me up once, mate, but I am all past that now. If she wants me to give her one, then that is what I do, no strings attached. I don't care if she does or doesn't come back but, if it helps you, then I will be fighting your corner, mate, to get her back here. Too right, I will."

We shook hands and he left. I ordered another lager. It was closing time when I staggered home from The Duck in an absolutely paralytic state. I stopped on the river bridge, as I had that afternoon. I was looking like a man who had lost everything, which basically I had. Much as I loved being a Listener, I would have given that away if only I could have Nicola back. I missed her already and I loved her very much. I was staring down at the black water of the river swirling in small whirlpools as the current grew stronger. *No one would stand a chance in there,* I thought, as the temptation to jump grew within me. Anyone falling in there by accident or design would be dragged under by the current. *Oh God, what will I do?* I felt hopeless, helpless.

I sensed someone standing next to me. It was a young policeman in full uniform. He looked at me and said, "Are you alright, sir?"

I gave a startled shudder, like a frightened rabbit. I was all nerves. I pulled myself together.

"Yeah, I'm alright, officer. Don't worry, I ain't jumping tonight."

"I hope not, sir. Why don't you walk on home now or I can call a cab for you, if you want one."

"No, I will walk. Thanks anyway, my friend." I walked on over the bridge and up the slight hill towards home.

I fell into my chair as I arrived back in the apartment and I sat there all night and all of the next day. I went out to the local convenience store on Wednesday evening and picked up four bottles of wine and a half bottle of brandy, along with some milk bread and a pack of cheap Irish sausages. I went back and sat in the chair. I stayed there for three days, only going out to top up with wine, beer, bread and sausages. I neither washed nor shaved, and my beard was starting to grow and the shaking of my hand became worse. I didn't care how I looked or how I smelt. I was beginning to feel that my mind did not belong to me. It was hard to figure out at that time but I felt unhinged.

On Monday I decided to go to The Duck to see if I could see John or Jade, or even Nicola. I went out at lunchtime and drank until six o'clock. I saw no one I knew and neither did I speak to a soul, I didn't know anyone in there. I wondered how it could be possible to feel so lonely in one of the world's largest and most cosmopolitan cities. I began to hate it in there. I decided to wander home. I was depressed and I did not want to do anything, just sit in my chair for days on end. It was now a week since I had been dumped by Nicola and the Listeners, and I wondered about phoning Nicola. I decided not to do that. I had stocked up with copious amounts of booze and bread and sausages. I just vegetated there in my chair and I knew I had a serious problem developing with my mental state. I thought depression was setting in.

The following Monday, two weeks after I had been dumped by Nicola, I had tortured myself enough and I summoned up the courage and called her. The phone rang for a long time until she finally answered.

"Robert, what do you want?" she sounded tired and drawn.

"I wanted to speak with you, Nic."

"There is no more to say, Robert."

"But it's such a waste, Nic. We were great together."

"Yes, we did have a good time for a short period."

"So can't we get back together and do it again?"

"You lied to me, Robert. How can I trust you? I spent eleven years of my life with someone who lied to me and when I was stupid enough to start a relationship with you, you lied within the first week. What's that all about?"

"But I love you, Nic."

"I loved you too, Robert, so don't think that you are the only one who's upset about this and in bits."

"I'm sorry, Nic."

"Too late, Robert. You lied and that's it."

"I've been thrown out of the organisation."

"For fuck's sake, Robert. What did you expect? You lied to them; you broke all the rules. Of course you've been thrown out. Listen, I'm truly sorry that this has happened but I have to go now."

The phone went dead. I opened a can of Stella.

The weekend came and went and I was deteriorating fast. It was now early August, or so I thought. I didn't care what bloody day it was. I was suffering from clinical depression, I knew this, not only from my training but because I had attended various mental health courses. I knew what I was suffering from. Sadly, it's okay to carry out these self-diagnoses but it is a totally different game to snap yourself out of it.

I was stuck in a downward spiral of mental anguish. I was dying from the inside out. The symptoms of this mental turmoil were low self-esteem, loss of confidence and a terrible feeling of guilt. I was harbouring a desire to end my life and had difficulty in concentrating on anything. I couldn't even walk properly by then; I was slouching around with my head bent and my shoulders dropped and rounded. I was suffering from sleeplessness and loss of appetite. Alcohol had become my best friend and my worst enemy. I was in the shit, and it was all my fault. I knew all of these things that were destroying me and yet I could do nothing about it. I kept thinking that maybe I should go to the doctor and tell him. No, not really, I would come away from there with a prescription for Prozac pills or some other magic cure, and I didn't need that. I needed Nicola – but there was absolutely zero chance of that.

I looked in the mirror and the image that stared back was unrecognisable to me. Was this really me? I had a spiky, horrible, scruffy-looking beard. My eyes were bloodshot and red-rimmed, with dark shadows beneath. I was unkempt and smelly, but I didn't care. This was all my fault and I deserved this punishment. I had nothing to live for.

I decided to go to The Duck again to see if I could see Jade or John. I didn't want to phone John, I don't know why. I just wanted to see him, perhaps because he was the only person I had who resembled a friend right now. I did the familiar walk down to the town, again stopping on the river bridge. I had become obsessed with the river, and I leant on the bridge rail and looked at the dark swirling waters on this summer's day, and again I imagined the waters enveloping me and taking away the pain that was my life. I stared down at the water for twenty minutes or more and there was no young police officer this time to send me home. The people of Welford were in a hurry, going about their daily business. They didn't have time to stop and bother with an old tramp looking into the river.

The play that I used to watch from my window was continuing to be acted out. Only now, instead of being in the audience, I was one of the actors. The never-ending, interminable performance of life continued.

I didn't jump that day; I continued my journey to The Duck. I entered and people moved out of my way. Maybe they thought I was carrying something infectious or maybe my invisible illness, my depression, was making me imagine this was happening. I stopped and looked carefully. I was staring into space in a busy pub at lunchtime and no one was taking the slightest bit of notice of me. I wobbled over to the bar and ordered a pint of lager.

A familiar face appeared in front of me. It was John.

"Strewth, mate, you look bloody rough," he exclaimed, looking me up and down. "What have you been doing with yourself?"

"Oh, John, don't ask, mate." I was anxious to avoid talking about my own parlous state. "Can I get you a drink, John?"

"No, Robert, I don't drink. Just having a quick Coke before I go back to work. She's back. Jade, I mean, got back yesterday and straight round mine she comes. I must be fucking mad but the benefits are wonderful, too good to let go. I'm addicted to her. That fella, the Dutch bloke, he gave her 20,000 euros to get rid of her. She is awful ain't she? Anyway, I told her what had happened to you and all the trouble she has brought you and she says she didn't know what she was doing and she is sorry and she will come to see you. Not in here, at your house, so expect a visit, mate. That was the best I could do for you. Okay? Hell, Robert, are you alright?" He was looking worried.

"Yes, John, don't worry. Thanks."

He threw his drink back and shook my hand and was gone, a busy young man indeed and nothing like the picture that Jade had painted of him, exactly the opposite in fact. John seemed to me to be a hardworking, caring, ambitious fellow who sadly had a sexual addiction for Jade. And Jade was, by the sounds of it, addicted to sex all the time.

I was beginning to feel agitated in the crowd of people so I walked back home, stopping at the convenience store for the usual supplies. In addition to the wine, lager, cognac and a bit of food, I bought a pack of cigarettes and a cheap lighter. I didn't smoke but, at this time, I thought it would settle my nerves.

I returned home to wallow in my misery and filth. I fell in and out of sleep and I didn't know what day it was. I felt as though I was dying slowly, minute by minute.

Chapter Twenty-Three

I was in the depths of the engine room of the SS Canberra. We were below the waterline but we could still hear the bombs going off. Water is a wonderful amplifier. We were encased in a metal tomb and the engine control room held eight of us, all engineers. We would die together here in our tomb. No need for a burial at sea, we were ready made for it. The room stank of diesel oil, machinery, sweat, fear and cigarette smoke.

The chief engineer, a very pragmatic man, had rescinded the no-smoking ban. "Well lads," he said, "we've got those Argie bastards chucking bombs at us, so we might just as well die of cancer! Yes?"

We all lit up. We were clad in white boiler suits with white smoke hoods with plastic helmets on our heads, the same as brick layers on a building site wore; no steel military helmets for us. Her Majesty's Government could not afford that luxury for merchant seamen. When the bombs were falling, we all stood stock still. All of us wanted to hit the deck, it was a natural thing to do. But not one of us dared to show that weakness to his shipmates.

When we moved, we moved very slowly, with terror in our eyes, and we looked like spooks, all dressed in white moving towards a victim. Only here we were the victims. We had been under attack for two days, not all the time, they came and went and we stayed at emergency stations the whole time. When they did come, the bombs came with them and that awful bloody noise. We waited for one to hit us, a long and dreadful wait full of fear. There was nothing that we could do, just sit there in our tomb waiting for a bomb to strike.

When the bomb eventually did find us, it struck the engine room in a blinding flash, and the deafening noise of the explosion burst our eardrums and threw us all to the floor. A couple of guys were screaming, muffled screaming, we couldn't hear, deafened by the blast, and we all headed for the escape routes. The door was jammed and the water was pouring in. It was soon around my feet and then my knees. We were clawing at the jammed doors and then the second bomb hit us and we were plunged into darkness. The thick, black, acrid smoke engulfed us, choking us, and the water was up to my chest. I was deaf and I couldn't see. I had to get out, I had to escape this hell. I was swept off my feet as the water came up to my chin and it was peaceful and I was a deaf man who was drowning.

I struggled and fought to get out, I touched the floating bodies of my dead ship mates and I started shouting, "Let me out! Please, God, let me out!" I was in terror, screaming, clawing at the bodies then pushing them away in horror, my mouth full of oily, stinking sea water. "Please, God, get me out of here!"

I woke up.

I was sweating, shivering and sobbing. Tears were running down my face and snot was pouring from my nose. My knees were up to my chin and I held myself and hugged my legs. Sobbing as I breathed in the air, breathing in great lungfuls, I was alive.

I sat vegetating in that armchair and another day passed and I did not notice time.

It was early morning when I first heard the voice. It was a voice I recognised, one that had once made a great impression upon me. It was Tonia, my caller, of a couple of months ago. Suicide in progress, the charities called it. Was I now a suicide in progress? I wondered.

The voice was speaking quietly, saying over and over again, "I couldn't take it any more, so I ended it."

I shook my head to get rid of the voice. "I used to be what they call a player," she said in an echoing tone.

I kept shaking my head. Where was she? Dead, I thought, but now she had come back to life, to haunt me. "I rampaged through life grabbing big lumps of it and I ate it all up." The voice of that elderly lady droned on in my head.

It was much later in the day, early afternoon I think, that the voice started talking directly to me.

"You do not have to suffer, Robert. Come to me, my boy. I will help you. Come to me and I will be here for you, as you were for me when I needed you. You need me now, Robert. You need me, don't you? You know that you need me, as I needed you."

The voice continued and I shouted and screamed at my tormentor, "Fuck off! Where are you? What are you doing to me, you fucking bitch!"

I burst into tears. I cried and cried and I knew that my total demise was not far away. I felt very alone and desperate.

It was at the stage where I lost my ability to distinguish colours. Everything I looked at was black, white and grey. I had started to live in a monochrome world. I tried blinking hard to make the colours come back. No matter what I tried, I couldn't get rid of the monochrome existence that I now endured. I was stuck in a world of greyness, which really freaked me out.

I regained my composure and I decided what I would do. It involved making a phone call to one of my rough friends who hung out in The Rose and Crown, my other local, the pub I visited when I wanted to experience the rough and tough side of life. My mate's name was Shagger, for obvious reasons; he was up for anything and any shape or size would do him. Shagger was one of those blokes who could get you anything, and his type exist in towns and communities all over the country. You name it, he would get it. Tobacco, fags, booze, drugs, guns, anything, no questions asked.

I found his number in my phone and rang it. He answered straight away. "Robert. How you hanging, man?"

"Hi, Shag. I'm good, mate, are you in the Rosie?"

"Yeah, man."

"Okay, cool. I need some pills ASAP."

"What pills, Robert? I got some Spice here. That's a laugh, mate."

"No, not that, Shag. I need twenty Diazepam and twenty strong sleeping pills."

"Okay, mate. No questions asked. I will have them here for you at ten tonight, alright? In the Rosie, I will wait outside the smoking shed, dead on ten. Don't be late, Robert. It will be a ton. Short notice always costs more."

"No matter, I'll be there at ten with the wonga. Cheers."

"Yeah, see you there, Robert." He rang off.

I continued to sit in my chair in my vegetative state, feeling a full bag of emotions. I felt too tired to move. I felt worried about even going out to pick up the pills. I was thinking that my world had ended, or was about to end. The voice in my brain was talking again. "Pick up the pills, Robert. Take the pills like I did. You will feel better."

Everyone hated me now anyway. I couldn't win.

I remembered Brenda the Listener. "Filthy," she had said. Bryn hated me and Ryan hated me, and above all others Nicola hated me. I was a man wandering in a thick fog, disorientated and frightened. I had no destination, save one. Death.

I began to weep again. My mind was leaving me, it was leaving my body, I knew it, I knew that all the feelings I was experiencing were those of a clinically depressed person. I had been trained in this. Because I could recognise it in others, I could recognise it in myself. But I was unable to do anything about it.

I poured a glass of wine. The voice of Tonia was saying to me, "Drink, Robert, drink and swallow the pills. It will be so much better for you. You will have peace, Robert."

I left the apartment at 9.30pm for my appointment with Shagger. The Rose and Crown was just half-a-mile away, closer than The Duck. I was locking the upstairs door to my gaff when a familiar voice came to me from above. It was my neighbour Charles Dancer. My hearing was fuddled. He looked down over the banisters at me and said. "Good God, old boy, you look different."

I thought, *Oh shit, I really don't need this.*

"Pantomime rehearsal, Charles," I said, looking up at him.

"Pantomime? Good God. Who are you playing: Robinson Crusoe?" He was obviously referring to my unkempt and bearded appearance.

"You got it in one, Charles. Yes, I have the lead role in Robinson Crusoe."

"Well, I'll be damned. I thought you were. He was a scruffy beggar you know. Not Daniel Defoe. Robinson Crusoe was. I suppose you would be, living on a desert island like that. Anyway, you carry on, old boy."

The commander retired and turned back to his apartment, muttering, "Robinson Crusoe. I thought he was. Well I'll be damned."

I let myself out and shuffled slowly up the road. Everything was happening in slow motion. People were walking towards me like grey ghosts in slow motion. Cars were passing me in slow motion. The world was on the point of stopping. "How strange," I thought.

Shagger was waiting with the pills outside The Rose and Crown's smoking shed. The noise coming from the shed was very loud indeed, lots of laughter and shouting, and what I could smell meant that they were smoking more than just rolling tobacco in there.

"Thanks, Shag," I said as I took the pills and handed over the money.

"That's okay, Robert. Be careful with those, they can be fatal if you overdose on them."

Good, I thought.

I returned to my apartment and was unlocking the front door to the building when I heard a voice behind me. I recognised it immediately. Jade was calling.

Chapter Twenty-Four

"**R**obert, I know you are angry with me, but you must listen." She was running up the steps to the apartment block. She stopped dead in her tracks when she saw me. "Oh my God, what has happened to you?"

I was half inside the building and half out, and I glared at her. I must have looked like a wild man and my glare must have scared her because she stepped backwards as though to escape the horrific and threatening look I gave her.

"What's happened to me?" I yelled. I knew I was shouting but I couldn't stop myself. "What's fucking happened to me? You have happened to me, Jade. You have ruined my life! You bloody bastard!"

"Okay, Robert, let's go inside, I need speaking with you." She pushed past me and got inside the main entrance and ran up the stairs to my door, where she waited for me to catch up.

"Get out of here, Jade! You've done enough damage. You have fucked me right over!" I couldn't stop shouting.

I heard the door upstairs open and a voice called down from the landing above. "Are you alright, old boy? What happened to Robinson Crusoe?" Charles was leaning so far over the banisters I thought he was perilously close to toppling over. "Oh, she's back," he observed.

I couldn't put up with Charles's running commentary, so I unlocked the door and pushed Jade inside. I shoved her into the hallway, where there was a full-length mirror, and I caught sight of myself. My hair was uncombed and unwashed, my beard had grown, my white T-shirt had stains all down the front and my jeans were dirty. I looked like a wild man who had been shipwrecked, Robinson Crusoe in fact, long lost on a Pacific island. No wonder people looked shocked when they saw me. Jade made her way into my very untidy living room. I looked at her in what must have been a very intimidating way but she was unflinching in her attitude to me.

"You are in a mess, Robert, and I know I have caused it. John made me come here and I have to apologise," she said in a very contrite manner.

"Why did you do what you did? Why?" I asked, almost pleading for an explanation.

"I am not well in my mind, Robert. I don't know I am doing these things. I have a deep hatred of what I call white men." She looked so demure stood there in her white blouse and tight denim jeans. The large Jade stone was ever present on its gold chain hanging around her neck. "I have hated white men since I was twelve, when they first come to my orphanage and pay the monks and my uncle to fuck me and other young girls."

"I thought you had a family in Vietnam." I was curious now.

"No family." She held the Jade stone in her fingers. "I tell you about my grandmother. I say she give me this stone. I have no grandmother; I stole this from drunken Russian man. I cut his throat with a very sharp knife when he sleep after I tired him out and I cut and I cut. I take stone and all his money. I kill him and run away to big city."

The hatred for this imaginary Russian was emanating from the look on her face, almost as if she was reliving this horror she had suffered.

"I was born and abandoned by my mother; I never meet her. I live in orphanage until I was thirteen when I run away after white men pay monks to fuck me. My uncle was there also, he bring men to monks and they all use us. I ran away to Hue and live in this city in brothel and I now charge white men to fuck me. I hate white men. They cause nothing but trouble in Vietnam. First French men come and torture and kill, then Americans come with bombs and napalm. They killed fifteen million of my people in their war. The American war. When we throw them out in 1975 the white man still come to fuck young girl. White men are no good. When I come here, I make white men pay. Not only money but pay in their lives. I sleep with them and take pictures of them in bed with me and then tell wives. I hate them. I have had so much sex with men that I am now addicted to sex because it is the only thing I know. The only sex I enjoy now is with John, and he takes good care of me, he loves me."

"I did nothing to hurt you, Jade. I tried to help you. I never touched you."

"Yes, Robert, you were different. I loved you as a teacher, a counsellor, when you first see me in your office. No one has spoken to me like you did then. No one has cared for me like that and not want sex. Even John. I lied to you, but you show that you care. I wanted to see you again but you say no. Then I see you with your girlfriend and I am jealous. Then when I come here you don't want to have sex with me when all other men do, so I went crazy. I am so sorry about your cat. In Vietnam we eat cat but here I know you love them. I am sorry about your car, door and mirror. Then I am sorry for writing letter to Listening chief. John tell me that I must make all things right, so tonight I send a letter to the Listening chief. I take letter to door and give it to big man called Ryan with silver hair and tell him I am a liar about you. He said thank you and I tell him he must put things right for you. I will do anything now to help you."

"Thank you, but you are too late."

"It is never too late to make things right."

"Well, if you really want to make things right tell my girlfriend your story about me. Go on, tell her."

"I will. I will phone her, you give me the number. I will phone her in the morning."

I searched for some paper to write on and all I could find was a small brochure on my fishery. I wrote Nicola's number on the back of that and gave it to Jade.

"Phone her now," I said.

She was looking at the brochure and Nicola's number and she seemed deep in thought.

"No, I won't phone her now, it is too late. Not good time to phone anyone, especially this woman I must beg to." Jade was adamant she wouldn't phone anyone tonight.

"Please, Jade, I really need you to phone Nicola tomorrow and tell her the truth. Do you understand?"

"Yes, I understand and I promise you that I will."

"Okay, now you must go, Jade. I have your number and you have mine so we can keep in contact but you must leave now because I want to kill you for what you have done to me and Nicola and all the other things that you did. But, above all else, I want to kill you for what you did to me and Nicola, I hate you the most for that."

"Oh, I see. Well, you are a very honest man. I will speak with you soon."

She left quietly, closing the front door behind her and all I could do was live in hope that Jade would be true to her word. I would have to wait.

I sat in that wretched chair, not wanting to move, for the rest of the night and the following morning. I did sleep for a few hours. I drank white wine, of which I had a plentiful supply in the fridge. I had heard nothing from Jade or Nicola and I didn't even know if Jade had bothered to contact her; her track record for keeping her word was not good.

The voice of Tonia was back in my mind that afternoon as I sat vegetating, depressed and broken-hearted. The voice was willing me to take the pills I now had and join her in the heavenly place she now inhabited, and all my troubles would be over.

It was late afternoon when my phone finally rang. I jumped out of my skin. I thought it would be Nicola, but sadly it wasn't. It was Ryan, chairman of the Welford branch of the Listeners.

He got straight to the point. "Robert, I have to tell you that we have received another letter from the Vietnamese lady called Jade. In fact, she did call here to deliver the letter and I briefly met her. She was very contrite. Anyway, in this letter she is now saying that she lied to us about you because she is suffering from a psychotic illness. She says that she never told you about her prostitution and that you never looked at her breasts or suggested that you meet up for a drink. She says that you kindly took her in when she was desperate and you behaved like a gentleman in as much as when she got in your bed you got out. In short, she has admitted everything that you told us about her and has completely corroborated your side of the story."

I sensed that at last something good was about to happen and I asked, "Does this mean you will be reinstating me?"

"Although she has withdrawn a substantial amount, if not all, of the allegations which she originally made against you, Robert, it does not alter the fact that you still had dealings with a caller outside of the branch. When she first approached you in the pub you should have run like hell and reported it to me. The very first day that you met her in the branch and she asked you to meet for a drink you did not tell your leader. You should have told us of her visit to your house and that she was following you but you did not and, consequently, we are unable to reinstate you, Robert. You have made too many mistakes and have bent the rules too many times. I am very sorry."

I sighed at this and resignedly said, "That's okay, I understand."

I cut the phone off. That was that then. No Listeners and no Nicola. Surely I would have heard from her by now if she had wanted to talk?

Tonia, however, was talking to me again. "How much more can you take, Robert? No one is bothered about you, they don't love you. Come to me. Peace, Robert, is what you need."

I was beating my head with my fists to try to get rid of those bloody voices. It did no good. It was gone 9pm when I decided I had taken all I could take and I took out the pills. I wanted out of this world now. I remembered Tonia saying to me that she did not want the room to smell when she died and I did not want to die here where no one would find my body, possibly for weeks or months. No one ever came here. No, I had decided. I wanted to die in the open air and for someone to find me dead in natural surroundings, with no drama of kicking in the door. I wanted to die in a place that I loved. My fishery, that's where I would go.

I picked up the two boxes of pills and went to my sideboard and pulled out a vintage bottle of Remy Martin cognac, which I had been saving for a special occasion. Well, what better special occasion than my own death by my own hand. I took a final look around my apartment, picked up my car keys and left, switching out the living room light. I would never see my apartment again.

Tonia was telling me, "You are doing the right thing, Robert. End it soon, end your pain."

Chapter Twenty-Five

I drove to the fishing lakes. It was still light in that wonderful summer of 2017. I had been drinking for nearly a month now, but I didn't feel drunk. I knew I shouldn't be driving but in my tortured mind it was impossible to tell right from wrong. The journey was perilous but without incident. It was dark by the time I drove down the dirt track to the fishery. My drunkenness and the darkness caused me to take extra care down the narrow dirt track. There were no cars in the car park and I used the fob to open the electric gates, reaching out of my window to make contact. The gates started to open and I dropped the fob.

"Shit." I cursed. I had to use the fob again to close them behind me. The gates did not close automatically because anglers would have large amounts of equipment to hump through the gates and the management didn't want to crush one of their members.

I stopped the car and searched for the fob using a torch I kept in the glove box. In my drunken, befuddled state, I didn't see it and at one point fell to my knees. It had been a miracle that I had driven all the way out there without incident. I abandoned my search for the fob.

Fuck the gates, I thought. I left them open and drove into the fishery, after checking for any sign of other anglers. The place seemed to be totally deserted. I was beginning to have double vision now. Crawling around on the ground had not helped me. I was driving past the first lake and instead of turning right along the track I turned left and slowly slid down an embankment and ended up with my front wheels in the lake and the rear of the car sticking up on the edge of the track.

"Oh, hell!" I said.

I switched off the engine and tried to pull myself from the car, which was precariously balanced on a ledge close to the water's edge with the radiator actually submerged in the water. My foot slipped down the ledge and I fell into the shallow water. I was sitting in it with the water up to my chest. Fortunately, in August, the water was warm. In my intoxicated state I struggled to get out of the lake and just as I gained my footing, I fell back in.

I thought, *Damn it, I will do it here. I will take the pills here. So what? The end result will be the same*. However, the pills and the Remy were still on the passenger's seat. I swore and pulled myself out of the water, leaned into my car and retrieved my phone, which had been on charge, and the bottle of Remy and the pills. I walked off, leaving the car door open. Lighting the way with my torch, I walked to the next lake, where there was a spot ten metres off the pathway under a large tree that I chose to sit under.

"Are you ready, Robert? This is your time, you can find peace soon," the voice was saying over and over in my head. This time I did not beat myself to make it go away. I was beginning to love the voice, relying on it to give me the courage to end everything. I did not care any more about the voice. Let her speak.

"Speak to me, Tonia," I gently called out.

I opened the Remy and had a slug, took out the pack of Diazepam and took four of the pills, washing them down with the cognac. I looked at my phone. No one had phoned. What's the point in looking any more?

"They don't want you, Robert. They have left you alone to die. They all want you to die, Robert. They cannot help you in life and just want you to die. Do it, Robert. Do it!" The voice was shouting at me now, almost in despair.

My life was to end here. My mind was all over the place, I had no control now. The voices were rampant in my head.

Not only was Tonia shouting at me, but Bryn and Brenda were joining in, telling me I was a failure, a good for nothing.

"She was in a thong!" yelled Bryn.

"Disgusting!" spat Brenda.

My mind had been taken from me, overrun by my despair, my misery. Everything was lost. I took four more Diazepam.

I spoke to all the people who were talking to me in my mind but I spoke mostly to Tonia.

"I'm doing it, you see, this isn't difficult. I have only been here five minutes and I'm on my way."

"Come to me, Robert."

I could see her now, for the first time she appeared to me, beckoning me with her hands. I can see her clearly, this woman whom I had never met in this world, and she was calling me to join her in the next. She was just above my head, a silver-haired woman with a sad face wearing a long, flowing white nightdress. She was beckoning to me, calling me. "Come to me, Robert. You will have peace, Robert."

I knew that I was now finished, the end was close. I would go to this woman, whom I had once stayed with as she ended her own life. She stood there calling. I reached out, trying to touch her, but I couldn't. Like a bad dream, as I reached out she seemed to move further away. "Come, Robert," she called to me.

I looked at my phone again and dialled a number. I had not planned to do this. Something, some hidden power, was making me do it. I was making a phone call, not to the Listeners but to the Samaritans, no one knew me there. Was this really me dialling the number 116123? The phone was ringing. I was shocked that I was actually making this call to the Samaritans.

The voice in my head started again. "Speak, Robert. Speak to your friends. They will help you die as you helped me," Tonia was telling me. Her voice was intermingled with the ringing of the phone.

"I didn't help you to die, you fucking bitch!" I shouted at the voice. "You were already dying. I stayed with you." My head slumped down onto my chest and I dribbled sputum down my clothing and moaned in despair.

"Fucking ungrateful," were my last words to Tonia.

Then a voice came on my phone.

"Samaritans, can I help you?" said a man with an Irish accent.

I jumped, startled at the sound of a real voice. I wasn't ready for this and I wanted to hang up, but then I remembered how much I hated SNAP calls. I didn't want to be a SNAP call. I tried to speak but only a groan came out. Silence.

"Samaritans, can I help?"

"Yes," I said. "No, not really. Where are you?"

"Northen Ireland," answered the voice.

"Joo you," I started. I breathed in deeply and exhaled into the phone. "Do you like it there?" I asked.

"Are you liking it where you are today?" said the chirpy voice with a strong Belfast accent. I had sailed with guys from Belfast in the past, in another world when my mind was sound.

"No, not really," I slurred. "I'm sat under a tree."

"Under a tree?"

"Yeah, mate, under a tree." I took a slug of Remy with a pill. I wasn't any good at this. Tonia took loads of pills while she was on the phone.

"Do you mind if I ask, are you taking a drink?" the sing-song voice asked me.

"Yeah, mate, I'm drinking under the tree."

"Do you find that drinking alcohol helps you?" I hoped that I wasn't talking to some Northern Ireland Presbyterian lay preacher who would berate me for imbibing in the evil drink. I really didn't need that right now. Then in my drunken, depressed state, I realised that I was talking to a Samaritan. Totally non-judgemental.

"Not really," I answered.

"Do you reckon that you think more clearly without the drink?" I realised that this bloke was good. A good Samaritan.

"Yeah, I think more clearly without this shit."

"Then, please excuse me for asking but, why do you take the stuff that you call shit?"

"Cos I'm fucking depressed, that's why," I raised my voice. "Sorry for shouting, mate."

"That's okay. What made you phone us?"

"Tonia did."

"Was Tonia worried about you because you are depressed?"

"No, she wants me to join her in heaven and she told me to phone you."

"Are you saying that Tonia is in heaven?"

"Yep."

"She wants you to join her in heaven?"

"Yes, mate, she does, she talks to me all the time."

I dropped my bottle of cognac and fumbled around for it. I took a slug.

"When did Tonia go to heaven?" he asked.

"Month ago, maybe more," I slurred and belched. "Sorry, I fucking belched."

"That's alright, no problem. So, Tonia is still talking to you after a month."

"Yeah."

"So, Tonia is a voice in your head. Is that right?"

"Yes, she tells me what to do."

"Can I ask, does she want you to die?"

"Yep she wants me to die."

"Do you want to die?"

"Do I want to die? Well, yes, but if Nicola could be with me no then … no, then I wouldn't die."

"You're saying Nicola could keep you alive?"

"Yep, she could, I suppose."

"So, where is Nicola now?"

"Don't want me, she don't want me cos I'm a twat. I behaved badly and she doesn't like lying."

I blurted out these words. I was beginning to feel silly now. I needed to get on with what I came here to do.

"Okay, I understand. So you are ending your life because you upset Nicola and she no longer wants you and Tonia is telling you to do it? Is that correct?"

"Absolutely, mate, you got it." I took another gulp of cognac and I could feel my phone vibrating; someone else was calling. I looked and it was Jade.

"Is someone trying to call you?" the Samaritan said.

"Yes, it's Jade."

"Jade?"

"Yes, it's complicated, isn't it?

The phone stopped vibrating.

"It sounds like it. Yes. Are you trying to end your life now?"

"Yeah, I am. I'm taking Diazepam."

"Have you taken many?"

"Can't remember. Six or eight maybe."

"How many more will you take?"

"Dunno, the whole bloody pack I suppose. I got sleeping tablets as well."

"Okay, so you will take all of those tablets but you don't really want to be dead. Is that correct?"

"Yes … no. I told you I want to die, that's why I'm here in this place in the middle of nowhere."

"But if Nicola could be with you, then you don't want to be dead?"

"Not if she was back in my life, no, I wouldn't want to be dead then, no."

"So, you don't really want to die?"

"Oh, shit, that was a brilliant question," I mumbled.

"Okay. Do you know the answer?" asked my Irish friend.

I was silent a long time and I thought about what this Irish Samaritan was saying, and I could only agree with him. At the end of the day I didn't want to be dead if there was a chance of being with Nicola.

"No, mate. No, I don't want to be dead."

This guy had sobered me up somewhat and had, in his own indirect and non-interfering way, made me realise that I didn't want to die. I wanted Nicola, pure and simple. I needed to be with Nicola.

He answered, "Good, I am glad to hear that. What will you do now then?"

"I need to get my car out of the lake. Not now, maybe tomorrow. Now, if I have to … I will phone a cab to take me home."

"I need to say something really important. You need to think about getting yourself to a hospital because you have taken an overdose mixed with a lot of alcohol, and it could have serious consequences for you. Will you get yourself checked out?"

"Yes, mate, I will. Thank you."

My phone started to vibrate again. It was Jade. I needed to answer it. The Samaritan heard the ringing tone.

"Do you want to get that?" asked the Irish voice. "You can phone us back if you need us."

"Yeah, mate, thanks. Thanks a lot. I know about the Samaritans." I switched to accept Jade's call and cut the Samaritan off.

"Robert, where are you?"

"Under a tree."

"What you mean, Robert, under a tree?"

"Fishing," I blurted. "Where is Nicola?"

"I spoke to her, she hates me, but she is very worried about you now I tell her what you look like. Are you at that fishing lake?" Jade asked.

"Yes. How do you know?"

"You gave me leaflet with Nicola's number written on it."

"I'm here and I ain't leaving here alive." I was back in depression mode. Or was I trying to pressurise Jade and therefore Nicola?

"What you mean, Robert? Not leave there alive. Why you say this?"

"Cos I'm fucking dying, cos I'm no fucking use any more, not to anyone."

"You go crazy, Robert. Stay where you are …"

I interrupted her. "You made me crazy, Jade, you fucking did it," I was sobbing now.

"I am going to phone Nicola. Stay there, Robert. Nicola will know what to do."

She rang off.

"Fuck Nicola," I said. "Well I did, didn't I, loads of times."

I started laughing hysterically then I cried and cried, sobbing myself stupid. What had I done? *Oh God, I've been so stupid. I am ill, I know it, but now is the time to fight it, not surrender to it.* I sat there for a while longer. The phone rang again. It was Jade.

"You must to stay there, Robert. Nicola, she come now, I give her address. You stay there, okay?"

"Can't go anywhere," I said and rang off. Immediately the phone rang again I cut it off. I'd had enough. The voices in my mind started again. "Are you coming, Robert, you need to do it now."

"Fuck off," I shouted and took more cognac but no pills this time. I sat there and vomited all down my front. I was in a hell of a state. I did realise though that vomiting was good, it might get rid of some of the pills. The Irish Samaritan was right. I did not want to die.

Wet through from falling in the lake and covered in my own vomit, I wanted to sleep but I stopped myself. The voice in my head was telling me to go to sleep. Then there was a new voice. Nicola was saying, "Stay awake, Robert, or you will never see me again if you fall asleep. Stay awake."

I tried to stay awake. I started singing a song, 'Come Fly with Me'. I sang and blurted out the words. I tried to get up, I wanted to piss and I was nearly up when I fell again. I pissed myself. Pissed my pants like a child or a geriatric man, which is what I felt like.

This is rock bottom, I thought. I lay there cursing myself.

My phone was vibrating; it was probably Jade. I couldn't find my phone. I struggled to get up on my feet, pulling myself up, leaning against the tree. Finally, I was stood up, hugging the tree. I stayed there for a long time; it must have been more than twenty minutes. I couldn't move. I wasn't cold but I started to shake violently. I just stood there hugging my tree. I felt that the tree was giving me its life's juices, keeping me alive. I hung on for dear life, frightened to let go.

I remembered what the Irish Samaritan had said and I definitely knew I did not wish to die. I needed to recover and get on with my life. Nicola was coming to me. Did this mean that she wants me again? I doubted it, not in the state I was in.

Oh, Christ, what a fucking mess. I dozed off, leaning against my tree.

After what seemed like an eternity of dozing and waking, not really sleeping, I awoke with a jump and I could see the lights of a car approaching. I felt my phone vibrating in my pocket. I let go of the tree and fished my phone out of my pocket but it stopped vibrating, the caller had rung off.

The car lights were coming towards me and I waved the phone with its lit-up screen at the lights. The car stopped near my car, which was down the embankment in the lake. Someone got out of the car and ran down the bank, arms outstretched to keep their balance. Then I heard a panic-stricken voice. It was Nicola, and I breathed a sigh of relief as she called out.

"Robert, where are you? Oh God, Robert, what have you done?"

I shouted back hoarsely, "I'm over here, Nic! Over here!"

She obviously couldn't hear me and I saw her looking into my car.

"Where are you, Robert?" She sounded very distraught. Then I remembered the torch on my phone and managed to switch it on. I waved the torch. I did not want to die now. I wanted to live. I could see Nicola running back to her car. The car started to move towards me. It stopped ten metres from me, the door opened and I heard her voice.

"Robert, are you alright?" Her voice was anxious.

I couldn't speak. I just waved the torch. Nicola came to me and hugged me; I could feel her face wet with tears.

"Sorry, Nic," I said, "I'm covered in vomit."

"I don't care. I will never leave you again. Jade said you were going to kill yourself. Oh God, Robert, look at the mess you're in!" she cried out in despair.

"I'm so sorry, Nic. My brain, there's something seriously wrong with me. I have voices telling me to kill myself. I did what the voices said. I ..."

I couldn't talk any more. I just held onto this woman whom I loved, and hoped she could give me deliverance from the hell I had been through.

"Robert, come on, I'm taking you to hospital." She grabbed my arm and pulled me towards her car.

"I love you, Nicola."

"I love you too, Robert. Very much. But you are such a knob."

Epilogue

April 2019

All those events occurred twenty months ago. My brief spell of mental illness had shaken me to the core. Maybe I still suffer from the invisible illness, like an alcoholic who has spent many years in total abstention; the fact is that person will always be an alcoholic. The same may be the case for my mental illness, I may still have it, but it is under control and I live a happy and normal life with the woman I love. Nicola and I are still together.

When Nicola's divorce settlement was finalised, we decided we did not want to live apart and we moved into her new house together. I sold my apartment and we moved down to the South Coast, where we live busy, happy lives.

Nicola is now a Samaritan, working in a South Coast branch. I will never be able to return as a Listener; I was thrown out – and quite rightly so. I had breached so many guidelines that were only there to protect the callers. I am sitting the exams to become a mental health counsellor and I work with a charity that helps young people with mental health issues to cope with their problems.

Finally, I have not seen or heard anything of Jade, the Vietnamese prostitute and killer who had suffered so much in her short life. She had caused me so much trouble and pain, yet I often think of her. She did, however, get Nicola and me back together – and for that I am grateful. I'm just glad I will never have to see her again. Or will I?

Jade

Jade is beautiful. Jade is ruthless. Jade is irresistible. Jade is a killer. She is capable of anything.

When the love of Jade's life is driven to suicide by an unscrupulous multi-millionaire businessman, she vows to take revenge. Using her all too obvious charms she embarks on a single-minded mission to destroy the men who have destroyed her life.

Her journey leads her into encounters with criminal gangs and the British Intelligence Service.

Jade is back – early 2020

47040886R00137

Printed in Poland
by Amazon Fulfillment
Poland Sp. z o.o., Wrocław